DIRTY MONEY

Laundering $19M of Chicago Drug Money
Playfully, with Merriment

*"How Do You Spend It
Without Becoming an IRS Lightning Rod?"*

"Hold my beer…"

JARVIS ENDICOTT WILLIAMS

Publishing Services provided by Paper Raven Books LLC

Printed in the United States of America

First Printing, 2022

Hardback ISBN: 978-1-7379-1673-4
Paperback ISBN: 978-1-7379-1672-7

Visit www.jarviswrites.page for links to more books
by Jarvis Endicott Williams.
Or find them all on Amazon, Nook, etc.

Four more thriller/mystery/crime-fiction/suspense/
humor books, similar to *Dirty Money*,
are being published soon.
Look for the next one on Conch Key,
A Rum With a View.

Non-fiction books by the author are:
Feeding Your Dog and Cat, The Truth!
Prayer Lite

FOREWORD

Finding sunken treasure is not as fun as it used to be… especially if it's drug money.

The cartel wants it back. Law enforcement probes. Sunken boats cause the environmentalists to agonize and preservationists to contend. Discovery and NatGeo document. Media exaggerates. The Coast Guard takes steps. Insurance companies send experts. Social media virals. The captain is smeared. The boat manufacturer is answerable. Lawyers hold forth and lunch.

But…the biggest problem is…how do you spend it without making yourself a lightning rod for the IRS?

Two retired, barefoot, alcohol-addled, sunburned, confirmed bachelors named Endi and Coleman found ways. And they did it with glee and merriment…plus:

They never paid a cent in taxes. They never got a letter from a lawyer. They were never questioned by the authorities. They even ended up having the mob's protection. They weren't shot, spear-gunned, tortured, maimed, waterboarded, jailed, sued, or thrown overboard with their feet in concrete.

Besides having a hilarious rocking good time…

They never missed a cocktail hour.

They get unlimited free new mattresses for life.

They get free visits from the Stripper-of-the-Month Club.

They get free medical care, including cosmetic surgery.

They fly free anywhere.

They found homes for Somali orphans…and saved Haitian girls from the slave trade.

They were instrumental in the formation of an airborne hurricane early warning, and anti-smuggling, system between Key West and Cuba, supported by the U.S. Coast Guard.

But wait, there's more…they have lifetime access to world-class spiritual advisors. (Except, they don't take advantage of this because they are single, rich, and maintain their blood alcohol level (BAL) between .030 and .059 percent.[1])

They also…well, you'll have to read the entire account.

---

1 This is a blood alcohol level at which behavior modifications include being: mildly euphoric, relaxed, joyous, talkative, and demonstrating heightened pleasure sensitivity, decreased inhibitions, and increased creativity.

PROLOGUE

Ignacio carried a small duffel bag with a million dollars in it, his only luggage, onto the 737. He was headed home to Haiti, where they would never find him (or even dare to look—Chicago is one thing; Haiti is another). As the plane gained altitude and cool air blew on his sweat-soaked face, he eased his head onto the headrest and shut his eyes, a happy man. *Momma will never have to work again.*

Ignacio worked for an affiliate of the Chicago Mob located in Ecuador that specialized in money laundering. He was supposed to run the stolen thirty-foot twin-engine Sea Ray cabin cruiser the fifty-five miles from Fort Lauderdale to Bimini. Then, after the cargo was unloaded, he was supposed to sink the boat in a thousand feet of ocean, with other boats of the same fate.

The cargo was drug money. There were twenty, one-foot-cubed, waterproof, vacuum-sealed plastic bundles each holding a million in hundreds, fifties, and twenties. It was two weeks' profits from the Chicago Mob's St. Louis and Kansas City drug markets. The money was supposed to leave Bimini by air for Santa Clara, Cuba, then tour

Caribbean, East Indies, and Mexican banks for a while, where it could age gracefully, cleaning itself as it went.

Instead of Bimini, Ignacio cruised to Freeport, Grand Bahama, and helped himself to a cube. He and his mother were planning to get into the young girl slave trade. Not for prostitution. The girls would become nannies for rich Florida preschool through middle school little horrors whose parents practiced free-range parenting. Win, win, win.

Ignacio partially unscrewed a sea cock on the bottom of the Sea Ray's hull, and then gave the big white boat a shove into the outgoing tide. The plan was that it would drift west and sink in the mile-deep Atlantic Gulf Stream. After being pushed into the tide in Bimini, that's what would have happened. But the outgoing tide at Freeport sent it east instead of west.

The boat didn't sink because there was so much debris and sludge in the bilge that the open sea cock became partially plugged, so the boat did not take on more water than the bilge pumps could handle.

After drifting east, a hundred miles, to a position a half-mile offshore of a six-mile-long island called Conch Key, the batteries finally died, the bilge pumps quit, and the boat sank. It came to a rest on its side in thirty feet of clear, warm, Bahama water. Barracuda instantly trolled it looking for fresh human.

$ $ $

Many vessels over the centuries have been lost to the Conch Key reefs. In fact, the islanders, a large family named the Albrights, had made their living salvaging wrecked sailing vessels since 1775, when they first inhabited the island.

They abandoned their homes in New Jersey just before America's Declaration of Independence in 1776. They were loyal to King George, and pretty much had to get out of town fast. They wisely headed south to a warmer climate (as opposed to the idiots that headed to Canada). They wrecked on dead reef and, being stoic Puritans, made the best of it—God's will and all that. Before them no one had stayed on that island because it had no water, and was mostly impenetrable jungle with a few coconuts, a lot of sand, and completely untillable dead rocky coral. But it did have a lot of conchs to eat, and lots of rain to collect.

Being Puritans with little imagination, they called it Conch Key.

Conch Key residents nowadays aren't in the shipwreck salvage business anymore. Nobody watches the sea for ships in jeopardy like the old days. With GPS navigation and diesel engines, as opposed to sextants and sails, the incident of crack-ups on the reefs has been dramatically reduced.

Most modern-day boat sinkings now are for insurance purposes and are "salvaged" before they are sunk. Besides, the sinkings these days result in the boats disappearing forever into a "blue hole" that National Geographic has never found the bottom of, even after multiple attempts with more and more sophisticated equipment.[2]

---

2 In the last attempt by National Geographic, a remote-controlled submersible with camera accelerated as it dove and just disappeared. It is believed that a fast-moving river approximately one thousand feet below sea level gains speed through a series of narrowing caves via the Venturi effect and sucks down anything in its vortex, flushing it downstream to who knows where,

And so, our story is this: without causing attention to themselves, how do Coleman and Endi spend the 19 million dollars in hundreds, fifties, and twenties, that they found on the sunken Sea Ray? This was difficult because they really didn't have much use for the money anyway; you just don't need a Maserati on a desert island that only has golf carts, not one bar, not to mention a gentlemen's club, and they already had a year's supply of rum.

---

kind of like a toilet. It is believed that a network of blue holes may be the explanation for disappearances over the centuries in the area known as the Bermuda Triangle.

1

Coleman asked Endi, "You want another?"

"Is a fifteen-pound parakeet fat?"

"I'll take that as a yes."

Endi held out his glass with one hand. "Do we have a bedpan?"

"Good question."

Coleman stumbled as he reached for Endi's empty glass, and almost fell onto him lying in the hammock. He stumbled again over the door threshold on the way to the bar.

Endi said, "I'd think by now you would know all the stumbling points."

Coleman had inherited the house from his dad, who had bought it as a family getaway in the 1950s. Situated in the middle of a narrow six-mile-long desert island in the Bahamas, Coleman and Endi could watch the sun come up on the east, sipping coffee sweetened with rum…and watch the sun go down on the west side, finishing their daily bottles of rum, usually straight out of the bottle.

Coleman handed Endi a fresh drink and said, "No bedpan. Just go ahead and piss on the deck. We'll hose it off." The hammock was gently swinging between two posts that were part of the covered deck that went all the way around the house.

Endi rolled unsteadily onto his side, lowered the waistband of his bathing suit and tried to arch it off the veranda. Elderly prostate: a four-inch curly-tail lizard boiled from under the deck and shook its fist at Endi.

"Well, that's better."

"Atta boy."

Inspired, Coleman shuffled to the edge of the veranda. While peeing, his bathing suit fell around his ankles. He plopped down into a rattan-cushioned armchair behind him and next to the hammock. "We should dive that wreck." He struggled to pull his bathing suit up one handed (drink in the other) without having to stand up. Finally, he just left it around his ankles.

Endi let one leg flop out of the hammock and almost rolled out after it. "I'd give my right arm to be ambidextrous." He wiped rum and Coke off his bare chest.

"Tomorrow we go to the big island and fill the dive tanks."

"I need some Scotch for bedtime too," Endi added.

Conversation died. Occasional deep breath; satisfied sigh. Coleman's arm hooked over the back of the chair. Endi's laced fingers behind his head in the hammock. Coleman leaned to one side, allowing a fart its freedom. Unforced chuckles.

A gentle breeze smelling of hibiscus, gardenia, saltwater, and jungle fondled their bald heads. They felt nothing but endorphins, eyes half closed, lidded looks of satisfaction.

$ $ $

An hour before sunset, they headed to the dock as usual. Coleman's cabin cruiser, the *Wet Spot*, bobbed in the crystal-clear aquamarine water at the end of the long dock. They could see conch and starfish on the shallow bottom. They threw bread crumbs to schools of fish that looked like they should be in an aquarium. A cloud was building to the southwest muttering *please let me be a tropical storm* under its breath, like all clouds do. They made another drink from the cruiser's bar.

They watched the sun go down on the other side of the property sitting on the sun-warmed sand beach with their legs stretched in front of them. As they sipped their drinks, the warm ocean fondled their toes. Very few thoughts crossed their minds.

Sundown finally, yellow bug lights dimly lighting the veranda, they ate conch bisque, crispy French bread, polished off their daily bottle of rum, and listened to Barometer Bill's weather forecast on VHF.

They turned on the air conditioners in their respective rooms and slept through a rancorous tropical storm that tried to damage something, but just couldn't get up to speed.

2

The recently sunken Sea Ray, the *Master Baiter,* was deep enough that the waves above her didn't affect her at all. Coleman thought she looked peaceful…like she seemed relieved to have finally succumbed to what she had fought her whole existence—sinking. Fluids escaped in small teardrops and drifted to the surface. Bubbles bobbled up. Rubber fenders drifted. A small oil slick dispersed in rainbows on the calm surface.

They were sure they were the first to find her. They had dived this same spot the day before, spearfishing and looking for lobster, and there was no boat there. They had tied a buoy to the sunken ship's deck rail to mark the spot and thus officially claim salvage rights. Endi opened the cabin door and three life vests popped out and lazily drifted toward the surface. They waited a little longer to see if a barracuda or shark might bolt to freedom. The two knew there could be bodies in the boat. They also knew they would be pretty much nonthreatening…i.e., dead. Consequently, they treated it as a crime scene at first—careful not to disturb anything. No dead found; the gloves were off.

They found nineteen cubes of money, approximately one foot per side, stuffed in concealed places. It turned into a competition Easter egg hunt; whoever finds the most bundles wins. Endi knocked Coleman's regulator out of his mouth with his flipper, causing Coleman to panic. Endi laughed so hard he lost his regulator too, and also panicked. Escaping compressed air from their regulators blinded them further. (Of course, they recovered the mouthpieces, or the story would have concluded at this point.)

Back on their boat, they accused each other of intentionally pulling each other's breather off. Endi missed Coleman with an empty Kalik beer bottle, and Coleman missed Endi with a flipper. Both projectiles sailed off the boat. Their thoughts turned to the cube of money they had brought up with them.

Endi said, "Someone is going to be looking for this boat; or knows it's here because they sunk it and are planning to get the money later. Or sooner. We probably should put this back; or just throw it overboard right now. This boat wasn't running drugs; it's a Wells Fargo Armored Truck. Was she supposed to become an underwater ATM? Or a savings and loan? Like intentionally sunk? Does it belong to someone on the island?"

Coleman said, "I wonder if there are other sunken ATM boats?"

Endi said, "The island never has attracted organized crime." They both knew that even though it had no police force, the average well-to-do organized criminal wouldn't like it. It didn't have a liquor store, bar, casino, or a strip club. No dog or horse racing. No politicians to bribe. No judges to own. No

Italian bistros. Nobody to shoot. No place to wear high heels and diamonds, or Rolexes and tuxedos. Besides, every single person knew what every other person was doing moment by moment on this island. And there were four churches."

Endi said, "Let's go back down and get the rest."

They were low on air.

Endi: "I know where some scuba tanks are."

"Not at the mattress queen!" Coleman pleaded.

Endi: "Well it's that or a trip to the liquor store island for a tank fill. Maybe she's in Fort Lauderdale and we can break in and grab a couple of tanks with no one the wiser." (Actually, they could walk in because no one locked their doors on Conch Key. They didn't even shut them.)

Coleman: "If she is there, we abort."

The ex-Mrs. Serta was unsteadily standing on her paddleboard thirty feet from her dock in the island's protected harbor. She was basically on a surfboard with a long paddle. Paddleboards had become the rage to the complete astonishment of 99.999999% of the population of the world. The progress made on one was continuously compromised by frivolous waves, breezes, and wakes—what progress there was—as you were lucky to get up to one-quarter knot with a tailwind. It was damn hard not to fall off.

She had divorced Mr. Serta III two years ago. She got the house on Conch Key. Her maiden name was Finklestein. She insisted on being called Padme (it was really Gerta— Gerta F. Serta). Mr. Serta III found that what had attracted him to her at first, became tedious by their one-month anniversary. That was…her composite spirituality that capriciously ruled her life, depending on her mood at the moment. Jewish family values were salted with a dogma run over by karma, the "many rooms" of the Judeo-Christian "mansion," stars and crystals, Buddhist prayer flags, meditations, horn blowing, drumming, chanting, and a never-ending supply of itinerant leech spiritual advisors. "There are many roads to God," was her personal mantra. She apparently never tired of taking yet a different road. Some were not paved; some had washouts; some had high, fearsome bridges: so, she got off those roads at the intersections, off-ramps, and Ys, never staying on any road for very long. (She had an aggressive case of adult ADHD. "Pop-spirituality" is perfect for that condition.)

To Mr. Serta III, Padme was basically a cute, but tedious, pet that whined a lot and took a lot of upkeep. About all Mr. Serta III could say about her in a favorable light was that she was housebroken. That was more than could be said of her poodle, Ohm.

Ohm was on the paddleboard with Padme and immediately started barking hysterically at Coleman and Endi.

"Shit, she's home," Coleman said reversing the engines. "Abort. Abort," he said without his lips moving.

Padme Serta had taken an instant interest in Endi on the ferry from the liquor store island to Conch Key three months before. (Any new Caucasian male was interesting to Padme.) Endi had taken an instant interest in Padme as well; long, thick, streaked, surfer-blond hair and a tanned healthy body so small that his head filled with an instantly-love-at-first-sight image of him on his back, holding her by the waist, and bouncing her up and down on his dick. No one knew her age, but she could pass for nineteen. Her sleeveless short sundress blew in the wind with no regard to modesty, and by the time the ferry had reached Conch Key Endi had pretty much seen everything the oblivious (not really—she knew exactly what she was doing) Mrs. Serta had to offer. He was besotted. When he got her in bed the next day, she was so petite she hardly made a dent in her Posturepedic.

Endi tried to end it as fast as it had started. She, of course, was needy, possessive, high maintenance, and high drama. She never acknowledged that the tête-à-tête was over, much to Endi's consternation and Coleman's hilarious amusement. Coleman had been the object of her OCD fixation briefly once, which he had managed to fight off without getting involved at all, her failure resulting in her permanent bilious distain for him. No man had *not* wanted her since she was thirteen.

Fortunately for both guys, Padme spent a great deal of time at her Fort Lauderdale condo playing golf in tiny tennis skirts, with her divorced friends, nibbling appetizers and downing fruity drinks in designer bistros on Las Olas Boulevard.

"Endi," she screamed like a little girl when she saw him as he ducked below the boat sides. She began paddling the surfboard furiously toward the cruiser at one-half knot. She even left a tiny wake.

Coleman said, "Hey Padme," as she came up next to the cruiser.

"Hi Coleman," she said icily. "Shut up, Ohm."

The dog dove in the water and swam for shore. He knew he wasn't going be number one in bed for a while since men just showed up, and…that this was a good time to empty his anal glands on it.

"Hi Endiiiiii!" she giggled with a toss of hair, a shimmy, a paralyzing smile, and a highway-orange bikini butt wiggle. His brain went thud into his groin. Among many wonderful things she was during sex, she was especially vocal. Nothing turned him on more than a vocal woman. He felt a spasm.

He said, "Hey you. Wanna come aboard?"

Coleman groaned.

She hopped aboard and Endi pulled in the paddleboard. She smashed her body against his and kissed him hard, sticking her tongue deep into his mouth. She tasted salty and sweet and fruity, like the margarita she'd just had. She patted his crotch lightly and smiled and winked. Endi's balls climbed into the breech in preparation to fire.

"What you boys been up to today? Got anything to drink?" She spied the cooler and grabbed a Kalik beer. She put the cap of the long neck on the edge of the cooler and hit the top with a fist, popping the bottle cap. She drank half, wiped her mouth with her forearm, and said, "I was severely dehydrated—you are a lifesaver." She drank the rest and belched loudly with a grin. For a small girl she could really drink.

"And what is this?" She whipped the beach towel off the cube of bills wrapped in plastic. "Where in the hell did this come from?" Neither Coleman nor Endi said anything. They just looked at each other. She sat on it. "Well?"

Coleman whispered to Endi's ear, "I have an idea."

Thus, they had a partner who really knew how to spend money.

Gerta Padme Finklestein Serta acted fluffy, but just under the surface was a shrewd Jewish temple money changer.

3

The next morning the three motored back out to the wreck. Padme had supplied two full scuba tanks.

Coleman stayed on the *Wet Spot* to handle the boat and take the bundles from the divers. The bundles weighed around twenty-five pounds each, so the process was relatively easy and took less than forty-five minutes. Endi took the buoy off the sunken wreck that marked its location.

They dropped Padme off at her dock. She wanted a bundle. She wasn't hard to convince not to take one when the term drug lord was mentioned. In fact, she decided that she and Ohm would head to Florida the next day… with $10K.

The guys declined an invitation to come in for drinks. They pointed the boat toward Coleman's dock.

"You think she can be trusted?" Endi asked. His man-brain had quit its preparation, and his balls had dropped, so he was thinking clearly again.

Coleman answered, "She has more money than ten of us put together. Since she has so much money, her spending money won't raise any eyebrows. If she spends money on expensive stupid stuff, no one will be surprised. She can be our money laundering mistress."

Endi: "We should have stayed for drinks. What else we got to do today?"

Coleman: "Well for one thing, we got to hide the money, dumb-ass."

$ $ $

They waited until dark to move the bundles from the boat to the house.

They re-sank the waterproof bundles in the five-thousand-gallon cistern under Coleman's house.[3] Coleman locked the hatch above the huge water tank.

Coleman: "The drinking flag is raised."

As their BALs rose, their imaginations soared exponentially. They had a new project.

---

3 The island has no water (hence the name "desert island"), so each house collects rainwater from their roofs in gutters and stores it in cisterns dug in the coral under their houses. The tons of stored water additionally act as ballast during hurricanes. Between the ballast and the upside-down boat hull–shaped roofs, wind just passes on by. In fact, the hull-shaped roofs actually are pressed down by the wind. Carpenters on the island all have boat building in their DNA. Who knows what else is hidden in these cisterns all over the island?

4

Endi: "Let's buy a titty bar."

"Absolutely. I love perfumed and powdered thighs around my head," Coleman said with eyes closed and a deep sniff. He made a motorboat noise and shook his head with his tongue out as if he were between boobs or legs.

Endi: "Except I never want to work again."

Coleman: "How about we just do the talent scouting and auditioning."

Endi: "And costume design."

Coleman said, "Do you have any idea how much trouble we may be in? Some South American cartel is probably pinging right now…or will be. We should have checked the boat for a locater beacon of some kind."

Endi said, "Aw, cheer up. It's a big ocean. They'll never find it. Unless they sunk it there of course."

Coleman: "That's what I mean. Maybe we should re-float it in the middle of the night and tow it to the blue hole and re-sink it."

Endi: "How the hell do you re-float a boat?"

Coleman: "It would be epic to blow it up underwater." His thoughts faded trying to think of the anatomical term *pancreas*.

He was convinced that he had signs of early Alzheimer's, so without notice he wistfully practiced his recall skills. He would randomly try to remember something he knew that he knew, to test himself. He couldn't remember *pancreas.*

Endi was accustomed to Coleman's periodic drifting off. "Ok, what are you trying to think of now?"

Coleman vacantly replied, "I really don't know."

Endi: "How are we going to spend all this money and not be a lightning rod? I got all kinds of red flags waving in my brain. Like are the bills marked? Is it a 'sting' by some government? Is there a shootout between mobs heading our way? Have we been watched? Is a satellite transponder in each block of money? We should take the shit to the blue hole and dump it with the boat. Dump all the money and get back to our retirement. It might save the island besides. If we found the boat, others will too. Whoever is missing that boat and the money is going to shake down this island…like slash-and-burn shaking down, looking for their money. Turn the island into a beach if they have to."

Coleman dully said, "Padme's not going to agree with dumping millions of dollars back into the ocean or blowing the money up. And we are not going to dump it because…" He jumped up with fists in the air like Rocky, and shouted, "PANCREAS! I can still remember!"

Endi: "Way to go!"

Coleman continued with his train of thought, "… because this money laundering project is a monumental challenge. And we love challenges."

Endi said, "I need inspiration. I am at my most creative at 0.025%." He pulled out a breathalyzer from the coffee-table drawer and blew into it. "I'm only at 0.012%. No wonder I'm not thinking well—my brain needs fuel for thinking and repair. I need more to drink."[4]

He got up. "Break time." He mixed rum and Coke for both of them. He drank his down and mixed another one, then returned to the living room and set them on the coffee table. They both took healthy swallows.

Coleman said, "We could put some of the cubes of money on the beach like they washed ashore. Like even on a different island. We could put them in different places so it looks like they floated in different directions. We could still keep two, one for each of us."

"They don't float. We'd have to keep three now. Padme."

Endi: "Hey, what about our enemies? Like give them a million in drug money and watch what happens?"

They grinned at each other, nodding their heads with wry smiles. They each withdrew quietly into themselves, deep into their grudges.

Coleman broke the silence. "Remember the marina that put a hole in my boat with a forklift and the service manager blamed it on a 'weak bottom'? It's ass end sunk—never was right after being speared by the forklift?"

"Of course, I remember. Water wrecked the starters, transmissions, electrical system. The service manager was 'connected.' He kept blaming the boat."

---

4 In the last twenty years it has been proven that the brain continues to grow new cells. The myth that you have only so many brain cells, and every drink of methyl alcohol kills a couple of hundred, was debunked by neuro researchers as complete bullshit. (Much to Endi's relief.)

Coleman answered, "And no lawyer would touch my case after they found out who they were up against."

Coleman: "I like it. If we give a huge chunk of money to that asshole service manager, and whoever this money belongs to would probably find out and would climb up our recipient's ass!"

And so, they hatched their glorious money laundering scheme. The cascade of events that followed was epic.

$ $ $

In the morning they fished a million out of the cistern, and with it between them on the golf cart, covered with a beach towel, they drove it down the Queen's Highway (the only road on Conch Key) in Coleman's golf cart to Padme's house hoping she hadn't left for the mainland yet.

She loved the plan.

5

Somewhere in South America, Levitra Alverez stood before the family don, his father-in-law, with his head hung low. A drop of drool from his open mouth landed on his canvas Top-Siders.

"Levi, all I ask is that you steal a boat every month or so and get some captain to take our money to Cuba. A Special Olympian could do that. Maybe ten times a year you have to do this one thing. This is not something you delegate. With GPS, autopilot, radar, and satellite weather, how hard is it these days to take a boat from Fort Lauderdale to Cuba? In Christ's name, it is done every day by the competition! This makes two boats you have lost. You know how hard it was to find your last botch job, and take it away from those ponytailed idiots on Key West without drawing attention to ourselves? God, why am I so cursed?"

Levitra said, "I delegated because that's what you do, Popi. That way I no get caught." He had suddenly developed a fascination with his stingy brim hat's brim that he was working through his fingers like a Rosary.

"You know if this was Africa, you would be the one I would send out to steal meat from the lions."

"What?! I'm afraid of lions. You can't be serious. They bite." Levitra had no talent for languages. Popi spoke English ostensibly to make his son-in-law practice his language skills, but really it was for his own amusement.

"Shut up. Alright get on a plane and go to Florida. Get to Fort Lauderdale. Find that boat and my money. Take Guido." The gray-haired don jerked his head over his shoulder indicating a large hulk of a man in a luau-flowered shirt and shoulder holster standing behind him.

Guido was a six-foot-four, 240-pound Italian, with a shaved head. His sleepy eyes popped open, causing his unibrow to obliterate his forehead. "Boss, I can't swim."

Popi said, "Shut up. Who said anything about swimming? Let's get a sense of urgency here. Chop-chop!"

"Chop-chop? What the fuck that mean, Popi? I don't like the sound of that," whined Levitra.

Popi rolled his eyes. "It's just an expression for chrissake. Stay with me here. GO TO FORT LAUDERDALE NOW AND FIND MY MONEY! COPY!"

Levi: "You don't have to shout. I heard you. Copy what?"

Popi: "It's just an express…oh, for fuck sakes." The Don pointed to the door. Levi and Guido slunk out mumbling to each other with their heads down. Popi followed them and slammed the big solid pine door behind them. He looked up and clenched his fists, "You think You are funny creating that moron and giving him a big dick my daughter likes."

He heard a knock and a doleful, "Popi, we need money."

Popi sighed. "Of course you do," he said to the door. He softly banged his forehead against the door three times.

"You all right in there, Popi?" a pained voice said from the other side of the door.

I hope he gets killed. It would be worth twenty million.

6

That afternoon the boys went back to Padme's place for cocktails and planning.

Padme was in a red bikini top and a tie-dyed rainbow-colored sarong that rode low on her hips. She was gyrating to whatever was playing on her earbuds. She didn't hear Coleman and Endi. She was stuffing a mattress with money.

She had sautéed some marijuana in butter that morning. The fat in the butter extracted the THC. She used the THC-laden butter in a batch of snickerdoodles. Ohm had had a period of intense excitability after his cookie, but now was dreamlessly passed out in the shade on the deck under a ceiling fan.

Bumping and grinding to the music, she screamed when Coleman pulled her earbuds out. "Jeeeeezusss assholes," she squealed breathlessly.

Coleman said, "What's shakin' sugar?"

"Can't you knock?"

Endi said, "I really had no idea people hid money in mattresses anymore."

Coleman: "We smelled cookies from the road."

Padme finished and sewed up the hole. Endi and Coleman helped her put its plastic shipping wrapper back on and sealed that back up with wide transparent tape.

Finished, she patted both of them on the cheek as she sashayed by toward the kitchen. "Let's have some cookies and milk."

$ $ $

They were drinking St. Pauli Girl longnecks and nibbling cookies when two Haitians driving the hardware store Ford Ranger pickup (nicknamed the "Rust-Ranger") arrived with a mattress. The Haitians were high. (There is no such thing as a non-high Haitian male in the Bahamas.)

The brothers accepted the offer of a cold beer. They talked about their dream of permanently anchoring an old mega-yacht off one of the thousands of Bahamian uninhabited islands and turning it into a nightclub. Like Stiltsville, that is now all that's left of something similar in Biscayne Bay off Miami. In the 1930s it was a hugely popular spot during prohibition: a cabaret with strippers, individual one-room shacks on pilings for whores, and of course booze, music, and gambling.[5]

---

5 Crawfish Eddie Walker built a shack on stilts above the water in 1933 during the prohibition era because gambling was legal one mile offshore. He built on the sand banks of the Safety Valve on the edge of Biscayne Bay in Miami-Dade County, Florida. Of course, he sold booze. Others built shacks on pilings and a colony grew. In 1940 the *Quarterdeck Club* was built—a large house on a barge and pilings. In 1962 a 150-foot yacht was grounded and turned into a social club with free drinks to women wearing bikinis. Today, what's left after multiple hurricanes is called Stiltsville.

The Haitian brothers had to leave Padme's in time to make the last "slave ferry." (Blacks were not allowed to spend the night on the island.) This actually worked to their advantage. They moved things around the neighboring islands using the slave ferry, and taking advantage of the fact that no whites wanted to interact with them in any way other than to get them to do stuff like pick up palm bows, trim hedges, rake sand, and supply drugs.

They exchanged mattresses with Padme and took the one with the money in it.

Endi and Coleman agreed that buying an old ship and turning it into a nightclub might be an excellent use for their newly found wealth.

$ $ $

The two Haitians and the mattress boarded the last ferry of the day leaving Conch Key to Marsh Harbor. A panel truck drove the mattress from Marsh Harbor to Freeport during the night. It was stowed on a small freighter that made the run between Freeport and Fort Lauderdale twice a week, which left early that same morning.

A Haitian driving a faded blue 1974 Suburban with four different tires picked the mattress up at the Fort Lauderdale docks that evening and delivered it to the Rent-A-Wreck rental car office next to the Fort Lauderdale airport. The money (now in Ziploc bags) buried deep in its stuffing was removed. The cash was replaced with more Ziploc bags filled with marijuana, mushrooms, cocaine, hashish, and amphetamines. The mattress was sealed again in plastic and returned to the docks.

The Rent-A-Wreck's washman (Haitian, of course) got behind the wheel of a twelve-year-old green Ford Fiesta from the rental fleet the next morning. He was dressed in a flowered muumuu and wore a huge brimmed straw sun hat with a long scarf attached to the headband that waved over his face conveniently at key moments. He wore a long blond wig and huge rhinestone-decorated dark glasses. He headed to the service center at Lightningbolt Marina and Lounge. He had a duffel bag addressed to a Mikael Salsiderstern, aka Macro Salsa, the service manager of the marina.

The following day the returning Posturepedic was back on the ferry to Freeport and eventually made its way back to Conch Key, where the Haitian brothers continued business as usual. Just another day in paradise.

7

After work Macro Salsa drove his black Escalade to the strip club as usual. He calculated his percentage from the day's receipts from the service center, Lightningbolt Marina. Not a bad day, he thought to himself. All of the jobs were accomplished in half the time that he charged for. Out of the thirty-two invoices he'd generated that day only three of them had actually required him to buy new parts. Most of the parts he needed he'd harvested from other boats in the marina, replacing the stolen part with the damaged part from the boat he was fixing. That way he had another job as soon as the donor boat owner found his boat didn't work. (BOAT: **B**reak **O**ut **A**nother **T**housand.)

Macro was born in Miami to a nice well-to-do Jewish couple sixty years ago. His brother was a doctor. Macro sold yachts, the default job for a well-to-do family's idiot son, until he had come upon this service manager's position ten years ago. He'd changed his name from Mikael to Macro… and Salsiderstern to Salsa; one less chip on the shoulder.

As service manager of Lightningbolt Marina and Lounge, Macro had discovered the incredible income potential of taking care of boats for out-of-town owners.

A boat owner wants to take his vacation on his boat, not on the dock, so the boat needs to work perfectly when he hops out of the cab from the airport. Boat owners are actually happy to hear from their marina service manager that he had detected a problem (through his incredible diligence) such as a battery that was waning, or a starter rusting, or a hatch leaking, and are delighted to pay the service repair invoice because just thinking about their boat gives them warm fuzzies. Especially if it's February in Boston and they are experiencing yet another snowstorm and dreaming about the Sunshine State.

There was a problem—his wife. He pulled the Escalade into the Solid Gold Gentleman's Club on Broward for a couple of doubles, and a lap dance or two. He lamented; sixty, with a barely used penis. He was an INCEL—"Involuntarily Celibate." He swore that his wife had gained her first extra hundred pounds the night of their marriage; like the next day she was a hundred pounds bigger.

Macro was not as stupid as he looked, although he didn't know a torque wrench from a socket set. He didn't have to know stuff like that to get the work done; that's why God made Mexicans, he had discovered long ago. They instinctively made dishonesty look like diligence. They acted completely trustworthy and polite, but accepted graft and corruption as just a normal part of life. They never complained and were grateful to be working. They didn't bitch. You could always blame them for anything. They never bragged. They never banged the customers. They didn't drink or take drugs on the job. They crossed themselves all the time. First thing he did was fire all the Haitians and hire all Mexicans.

He gave all his Mexicans a short one-syllable name—easy to remember and easy to shout: Buck, Nick, Butch… "Hey Sam , take this fan belt off this boat and put it on that boat, and take the belt off that boat and put it on this boat. Comprende?" That worked better than Jesus do that… Jesus do this. *They all seem to be named Jesus for chrissake!*

"Si, boss. Switch belts. Bien." The Mexicans never questioned his orders. It was just work—it didn't have to make sense, or have anything to do with high standards, making a difference, or job satisfaction. It had only to do with a paycheck and job security—the Mexican hierarchy of needs.

Macro played the part of the hardworking blue-collar working man for his boat owners. He wore shop clothes with his name on the shirt. Steel-toed work boots. Screwdriver and pliers in a holster. Surgery booties and latex disposable gloves in case an actual owner was present. Obsequiousness. Deference. Flattery. Smarmy.

Everyone thought he HAD to be honest-looking like that: three or four chins under no chin, a nose that had grown, not down, but up, like a hog snout. His eyes were sad and earnest. His dyed black hair made a perfect circle all the way around his head except for a bald spot that made him look like he was Friar Tuck. He always carried his arms out to his sides like he was carrying something and walked fast like he had a pressing task to attend to. He removed his ball cap ceremoniously whenever he was around women. His body was shaped like a pear. He had discovered long ago that blue-collar guys got tips. White-collar guys did not. He got tipped a lot.

If anything of the careless sort happened to a boat under

the marina's watch, he had a knack for explaining to the boat owner that it was an event that was just waiting to happen—an act of God. "You wouldn't want the hull to crack on your way to Bimini. Be thankful it was discovered here where we can fix it. Weak bottom. The forklift driver should be rewarded for acting so fast to get your boat out of the water before it sank completely. By the way, the starters, batteries, voltage regulator…need replacing due to water damage…but that starter was weak anyway…about to fail you in Bimini where it would cost you ten times as much."

This is exactly what had happened to Coleman's boat. It didn't take long to find out that the forklift driver was a college student nephew of the club hostess, and that the kid drove the forklift like a race car. And that he didn't work there anymore. One or two accidents that could be turned to their advantage monetarily are one thing, but one every other day with forklift damage is another. Coleman argued that no matter what the underlying condition, it had happened at Lightningbolt Marina. They did it. *No, it was a weak bottom.* Of course, their insurance company experts agreed with the predisposed weak bottom theory and refused to pay."

Pretty much every business in South Florida has an oversight and troubleshooting partner (organized crime) that took a percentage off the top. No different at Lightningbolt Marina and Lounge. If the occasional boat owner got uppity, Macro knew he had help when he needed it, even if it required out-of-town connections. These partners also laundered money, because of all the things a business doesn't want, it is the IRS as a percentage-off-the-top partner, because no one wants to pay taxes.

Coleman was visited by a broad-shouldered team representing the marina that carried a cease-and-desist order signed by a judge with an accompanying restraining order instructing him not to harass Lightningbolt Marina and Lounge anymore or suffer the consequences. *Don't screw with South Florida businesses that have connections in Chicago.*

$ $ $

The next morning the elderly green Fiesta tailgated a boat slip renter into the marina through the secured gate before it shut automatically.

A witness said a long-haired blond in a muumuu with a sun hat covering her face placed a duffel bag at the front door of the marina service office and got back in her car. The witness watched the isolated event as he waited to get into the only bathroom at the marina. He didn't think about it again until he heard that there was a million bucks in the duffel. He remembered that the woman was the ugliest black gal he had ever seen in his life. She even had a goatee. He told the investigating detective that that was all he could remember as the door to the toilet had finally opened, and he had a turtle head poking out.

When Macro opened the duffel bag and saw what was in it, he collapsed into his desk chair, which fell backwards. As the chair went down, he knocked himself out on the credenza behind him.

News of the money spread instantly. Two Mexicans raided the office like roaches with the lights suddenly turned on and ran out the gate with fistfuls of money. It took a while for

Macro to wake up. He re-read the message: *Congrats, Mike. Well done.* He knew he deserved the money, somehow, for his sixty long years of life's unfair torment. He had won it. Or it was a gift from a grateful customer. Or a rich relative had died. It was supposed to be a surprise. He was counting it when a mariachi band started playing outside.

Everyone at the marina enjoyed themselves immensely as the party unfolded. Word spread fast among the "live-aboards." Most were unemployed and so always available for parties. (This liveaboard community happened to be worse than the scuzziest trailer park in the world—most boats didn't even run.) Mechanics, dock boys, salesmen, detailers, even people driving by, joined the fun…there is nothing like a mariachi band to announce a party.

Macro marveled at the elaborateness of the planning and the generosity of his unknown benefactor. Not just a fortune, but mariachis and pizza!

(The IRS, FBI, and CIA didn't show up, each assuming the anonymous tips they had received were pranks perpetrated by each other on each other as had been often done so often in the past.)

When interviewed by a young female reporter from a TV station, Macro was laughing hysterically and giving away hundred-dollar bills. He was drinking sangria from a gallon jug. His shirt and pants were gone and he was in just a puce-colored Speedo and matching flip-flops.

A girl was Velcro-ed to his arm kissing him on the ear and cheek all during the interview. She had his duffel bag of money over her shoulder. She was the strippergram girl. As she had stripped out of her policewoman's costume, she told Macro the duffel of money was a commission. She had been told by her agency to tell him that the money was a commission. She also told him that there was more money coming; the accountants would get in touch with him in a few days. It flashed through his mind that they got the wrong man, but the stripper kissed him long and hard and left a small pill in his mouth. The ecstasy slammed into action. The strippergram girl was going to give this new relationship all she had. This was a once-in-a-lifetime opportunity—being in the right place at the right time. Fuck junior college.

"The first thing I'm gonna do is get a divorce," Macro announced to the reporter. "Why are divorces so expensive?!" he asked the reporter. Without waiting for a response, he said, "Because they are WORTH IT!!!" Har, har, har, har. He squeezed his new girlfriend and bounced one of her heavy boobs in his non-drink-holding hand. She giggled demurely.

"Cut." The newswoman shook her head and said, "Let's try that again."

They finally got him to not bounce the boob for a moment. He really had no idea what he was saying at that point. He'd given the reporter over a thousand bucks by that time, which he had stuffed down her blouse a bill at a time. A collage of the interview filmed by a bystander with a smartphone, with the mariachi band in the background, went viral on Facebook and Instagram.

Macro's boss, the owner of the marina, finally cornered him in the bathroom. "You win the lottery?"

Macro said, "No, it's a commission. I quit, by the way."

"Commission for what?" his boss asked bad-temperedly. He was ten inches taller than Macro, and a hundred pounds heavier. Marco was pissing with the Speedo around his knees. He could feel the big man's breath fluff the thick hair on his back. The bathroom was tiny. His boss said, "I don't like the attention we are getting. Where are all the Mexicans?"

"Well, ex-boss, it doesn't matter what you like, or don't like. I am rich and being rich means getting attention. It also means freedom. And freedom means I don't have to talk to you." Macro pulled his Speedos back up and turned around. "Let me show you what I mean. Follow me. What do you mean where are all the Mexicans?"

He led the owner to his new girlfriend, whereupon he pulled an inch-thick stack of bills out of the duffel and gave it to the big man. "Here is the down payment on your Mercedes. How much you want for it—name your price."

"Thirty thousand." (In the boat business, everything is for sale instantly.) He added, "There are no Mexicans here… even with a mariachi band playing. Where'd they go, Macro?"

"Done. Honey, would you take care of the man please?" Honey (he had no idea what her name was) carefully began counting out hundred-dollar bills. She had to start over multiple times. She admitted that she had never been good at math. Macro's boss finally took over and threw his Mercedes keys into the duffel bag. He'd grabbed over sixty thousand. (In the boat business, everyone…)

Macro was skipping toward the just-arrived margarita truck.

$ $ $

The marina owner left the Mercedes and made a phone call as he drove a marina work truck out the gate.

"This is Pinky," a gravelly voice answered.

"Pinky, this is Boner."

"Bonadonna, how u doin?" Pinky Blitz asked "Boner" Bonadonna. "What's all the party-ian going on over to your marina?"

"You heard already?" Boner asked surprised.

"I have many ears and eyes and noses. Some jerk got a bag of money. You calling me for what reason?" Pinky asked.

"I think this smells. This asshole don't know where this money came from. Who is setting me up, Pinky? I bet every single bill in that bag of money's got cocaine on it. I'm bringing you some of it to look at. Competition must be screwing with me—trying to implicate me with someone else's drug proceeds. I know this is hot money. I'm surprised the feds aren't sniffing around. Or maybe they are. Party got to have a hundred there now. Or it's counterfeit money. It ain't you, is it?"

Pinky answered, "I don't go around giving away bags of money to stupids what work on boats for a living."

Boner: "Besides all the Mexicans are gone. They sense trouble; they run away."

Pinky: "Boner, your trouble better not be headed my way."

Boner: "I'm on my way to your place to pool our resources. That's why I'm calling. I'm gonna kill that toad Macro."

Pinky: "I'll tell Fat Tony to let you in."

8

Coleman and Endi had commandeered Padme's condo in Fort Lauderdale as the supreme headquarters for the allied effort. It was perfect. Four bedrooms, four baths, two kitchens, view of the Intracoastal Waterway, pool, minibars, maid service—gated with a security guard. Padme also had a minivan (for moving mattresses around).

Endi: "I wonder how our first bequeathment was received at Lightningbolt Marina and Lounge."

Coleman: "Oh, to be a fly on the wall."

Endi had tipped off the IRS, CIA, and the FBI about a massive amount of cash being delivered to a Macro Salsa, aka Mikael Salsiderstern, at the Lightningbolt Marina and Lounge in Fort Lauderdale. Coleman also sent three pizza deliveries with enough for seventy-five, an ambulance, the fire inspector, three wreckers, a mechanical bull, the sheriff's department, cable TV repair, Channel Seven Action News, AT&T, DISH, two funeral homes, and the local paper news team. All were supposed to get there around the same time.

It became a contest between Endi and Coleman to see who could come up with the most imaginative deliveries.

Coleman sent funeral arrangements from ten florists

with the same message: *Even a blind dog finds a bone every once in a while—congrats*. And a sangria party truck. And a beer and margarita truck with taps on the outside. He booked the "Rodeo Kids" trick rider horse show, which set up their performance on the grass around the marina's pool.

Endi sent animal control, telling them Macro had a pit bull that mauled an old lady. He sent three evangelical outfits saying Macro was dying and asked to be saved. He told PETA that a naked woman was riding a manatee. He sent three street-food trucks: Slap Yo Mama, Shrimp Pimp, and The Greasy Wiener. No budget; feed everybody.

Endi asked: "Did you find a band?"

Coleman: "Of course. The Instant Mariachis. Ten-piece. Told them it was a surprise party and just arrive in full costume and set up in front of the marina office and start playing with no warmup. Good thing about mariachis is they don't need electricity."

Endi: "Mariachi bands never need to warm up either; they just start with each musician in whatever key he wants. I wonder if the mariachis will be annoyed when the Marching Cobras all-black high-school drill team shows up."

Coleman: "I'm sure they are all professionals. Strippers?"

"Several."

Coleman: "You suppose someone is going to wonder where that much money came from?"

Endi: "Is a fifteen-pound robin fat?"

Coleman said, "It's our farewell performance, and I hope the first of many."

Endi said, "The suspense is terrible. I hope it lasts."

9

Popi screamed into the phone at Levitra. "That's my money. At the marina. I bet that is my money. I want my money. What are you doing about it? Where are you, you moron? You shit-for-brains? I'm going to be the laughingstock of all the cartels. Are you there, ass-breath?"

Levitra answered meekly, "Si, Popi."

"Speak English, you fuck-stick."

"Of course, Popi. Why though, this is Florida?"

"Because you need the practice. Your English isn't worth a shit, dick-breath."

"What means dick-breath, Popi?"

Silence.

"You there, Popi?"

"Jesus."

Levi: "Dick-breath means Jesus. Got it."

Popi: "Mother Mary Christ."

"Dick-breath means all that too, Popi? A religious term. I get it."

Silence. Silence.

"You there, Popi?"

Popi: "Ok, Levi. Read my lips. Go to the Lightningbolt

Marina there in Fort Lauderdale and get my money, capture the asshole that has it, and find out where he got it and what he did with the boat and where the rest of the goddam twenty million is." Popi sighed into his phone.

Levi: "How can I read your lips from Fort Lauderdale? You are at home. Am I supposed to be on Skype?"

Popi: "I'm coming there. Sit—stay. Don't move. Don't do anything."

Levi: "Can I go to the clubs. I don't get to Florida often."

Popi: "Fine. Don't speak Spanish. Don't get laid…SON-IN-LAW WHO IS MARRIED TO MY DAUGHTER. Get drunk. Take some drugs. Lose your passport. Get run over by a sightseeing bus. Don't even get a handjob."

Levi: "I didn't catch all that, Popi. There is a bus that I can get laid on?"

$ $ $

Levi and Guido drove their rented fire-engine-red, gold-trimmed Bentley convertible into the Lightningbolt Marina and Lounge. The electronic gate had been torn down and dragged onto the grass.

"It's a festival!" shouted Levi with glee. They had been cruising hoping they would stumble onto a titty bar and heard the mariachis as they drove by. "Where are all the old ladies on their knees with rosaries?" He assumed it was a religious festival as that was all they had that resembled this in Ecuador.

The sign at the entrance to the marina said "Lightningbolt Marina and Lounge." A little gong went off in

Levi's brain, but he didn't make the connection. He'd written down Popi's instructions as to which marina he was supposed to go to but had left them in the suite. He tried to think but nothing happened.

Guido answered, "I don't know, but I see TITTIES!"

Three giggling topless girls jumped in the Bentley and perched themselves on the top of the backseat waving and blowing kisses as the car rolled through the marina. A parade formed behind them.

The impromptu parade snaked through the marina and adjoining RV park led by the Bentley. Guido and Levi each had scored a liter pitcher of frozen margaritas. One of the dock boys picked up a large pontoon boat with the marina's giant boat forklift and joined the parade with the mariachis on board the pontoon boat. A pickup truck filled with revelers dragged four creepers with "water-skiers" holding on to ski ropes. A fishing boat on a trailer was towed behind a truck, with outriggers on the boat deployed and an entourage of "fishermen" on board casting and trolling the asphalt.

Levi asked the girls what the party was about.

"Some guy won a million dollars."

Levi's chest went "ping." All he could see was Popi's face glowering at him. This was the marina he was supposed to find.

He stopped the Bentley. "Get out!" he shouted at the girls. They fell over each other tumbling out of the car now modestly holding their arms over their bare breasts.

It didn't take long to pinpoint their target. Macro Salsa was dancing on top of the margarita truck. Naked. He was bruised and bleeding from a dozen spots. The ecstasy had made him impervious to pain. He was really dancing well; but of course, he fell off. Guido picked him up and fireman-carried the new millionaire to the Bentley and threw him in the back seat. Levi sat on him.

Guido went back into the mob and found a near-naked girl in high heels carrying around a duffel bag. He stopped her and asked her what was in it. She said innocently, her eyes completely unfocused, "a million dollars."

"Mr. Salsa requests your presence in his new convertible." He thought maybe she was blind because she just looked through him. He waved his hand in front of her face. She didn't blink. She followed him to the Bentley, and he put her in the front seat. As they left the marina, she threw money at people who parted to let the car by. Guido cracked her on the head with an empty Dos Equis beer bottle. "This drug business is completely out of hand."

They put the top up on the Bentley. Nobody missed Macro—the party continued without him. Except for his wife. She heard about the money on CNN. She could swear that it was her husband on top of a truck naked, dancing the Lambada. The station had made his genitals blurry. She recognized the band of hair around his head and his pig nose. The headline under the video read, *Local Marina Service Manager Wins a Million!*

The next short video featured her husband announcing to the camera that he was going to get a divorce and buy a strip club. She wagged an angry finger at the TV and said, "And I'm going to get a lap band. And a big-dicked coal-black Haitian…you piece of shit pencil dick."

10

"Popi, I find your money." Levitra was excited.

"No shit?" Popi was dumbfounded.

"And I have the thief, and his girlfriend accomplice. Both are tied up in the trunk of my rental car. What do you want me to do?" Levi was lying on the king-size bed in the master bedroom of a two-bedroom suite on the top floor of the Riverside Hotel on Las Olas Boulevard. He balanced a Bud Light on his chest and had just smoked a one-hit of hashish and had polished off all of the little bottles of booze from the minibar.

"Where is the money?"

"In the trunk with the thieves, Popi."

Popi: "How much money did you recover?"

Levi: "Only a bag full. Not a boat full. Haven't counted it yet."

Popi: "Where is Guido?"

Levi: "In the car with the thieves guarding the money until I talk to you, Popi."

Popi: "I have a bad feeling about this. Where are you? Why you not with the money?"

Levi: "What? I am in my hotel room."

Popi: "Why did you leave the money, ass-wipe?"

Levi: "My ass is very clean. I swim a lot. The car doesn't have a minibar. Plus, I needed to talk to you where other ears are not seeing."

Popi shouted, "Go to the car and get the money. You don't let the money out of your sight. Tell Guido to take the thieves in the trunk to our safe house and dump them and gag them and tie them up. I'm on my way. I'm in Mexico City now. My plane to Fort Lauderdale leaves in one hour. Where are you?"

Levi: "Just a second, Popi. I have to get a pencil and paper. What did you say? I have to take notes."

Popi: "Go down to the car and give the phone to Guido. Now."

Levi: "What did you say?"

Silence. Silence.

Popi: "Go…to…the…car…and…tell…Guido…to…call…me!"

$ $ $

When Levi got to the parking garage beneath the hotel, he couldn't remember where he had parked the bright red convertible. He finally realized that he couldn't find it because it wasn't there. He figured Guido had taken it to run an errand. He decided to head for the pool. He turned his phone to airplane mode. He would call Popi back when Guido got back.

$ $ $

Nick "Zio" Civella worked for the Catanzaro family that represented the Chicago Outfit, the Teamsters Union, and the Black Hand Cartel in southeast Florida. He was a soldier for the mob. He took orders. He was loyal to a paycheck, wherever that came from. He had his own things going on the side. Zio had been sent to the marina; the missing money and boat was common knowledge in the underworld. He followed the red Bentley convertible. He whacked the sleeping Guido on the back of the head with a bar of soap in a sock.

He was glad the Bentley had a large trunk. The unconscious Guido just fit between Macro and the girl, who were both conscious. He rubbed his crotch: *Fucker's a heavy fucker—I think the fucker fucking hernia'd me.* He took the duffle bag out, and after looking inside, put it on the floor at his feet under the steering wheel. Zio phoned and lied to his boss/consigliere Joey "Doves" Catanzaro that there was no money, but he had some captives, and he was hopeful.

Zio found a secluded shady spot and counted the money. It was in bundles. He estimated that there was short of a million. He figured no one knew he had the money except for the three in the trunk; the strippergram girl, Macro Salsa, and whoever the large hood was that he had surprised. He also found the keys to a Mercedes in the duffel bag. He thought maybe the car that the keys went to was at Lightningbolt Marina. He decided it would be worth a look.

He drove the Bentley to an empty house his organization used for storing people and chained his three gagged hostages to eyebolts set in the concrete slab that the tiny two-bedrooms was built on.

He drove the Bentley to the Eller Drive entrance of Port Everglades. From there he drove to the F Building, scrolled for a number on his cell phone, called, a garage door opened, and he drove the Bentley through the building's door, and straight into a shipping container. He grabbed the duffle bag and got a cab.

He went back to Lightningbolt Marina and told the cab to wait while he got his car. He spotted a Mercedes, punched the key fob, it chirped at him, and he told the taxi to follow him back to the docks.

He drove the Mercedes into the container with the Bentley. The cab drove him back to the hotel where he picked up his car and went back to the "storage" house.

The Bentley and Mercedes found themselves in Dubai three weeks later. The next day, thirty-five thousand Euros were deposited in a bank account in Randers, Denmark, to begin its long electronic trek around the world and eventually into Zio's account in Saint Lucia.

$ $ $

Seeing opportunity and reduced physical suffering, Guido spilled the beans immediately to Zio that he was looking for a missing twenty million. Zio said he was too. Guido said that he had no idea why Macro got a million, but he thought it could be some of his organization's missing twenty million. That he, and another guy named

Levitra, his boss's son-in-law, had been sent by their boss in Ecuador to find a trail leading to the lost money.

Guido and Zio agreed that the money Macro had gotten had to be a "message"; and that only drug cartels had cash to burn like that. They knew Macro had been a target for some reason, and not just a random lucky recipient. Macro had been made a lightning rod that got struck by lightning. Or a lightning rod for the marina he worked for. Or both.

Zio concluded that neither the girl nor Macro Salsa had any idea of the big picture whatsoever, much less where the money came from.

Lightningbolt Marina wasn't one of his group's protectorates. He had to be careful. He did not want to start a turf war. No one needed that attention. Broward County was stable as far as organized crime was concerned. One client was not worth fighting for. There were bigger fish to fry, like the horse and dog tracks, the lottery, and professional sports. It wasn't just jai alai and boxing anymore; it was almost the Dolphins' turn to go to the Super Bowl. Besides, he knew the competition wouldn't spend a million on this kind of stupid stunt.

Still, Lightningbolt Marina was now on his radar, and sooner rather than later, he was going to have to find out why it, and Macro Salsa, was a target. He reasoned that whoever sent the money to this Salsa idiot: 1—It was not their money. And 2—It was revenge toward, or a message to, the marina, and Macro Salsa in particular. And 3—It was drug money belonging to some mob family. And 4—It was a rocket's-red-glare-and-bombs-bursting-in-air signal that whoever sent that million to Macro had that mob family's money. *In your face, assholes!*

More importantly, Guido said that there was nineteen more million somewhere. Zio said he wanted to retire to Ecuador, the best kept secret in South America. He wanted out of South Florida, and out of the business. He was sick of the soldier's life. He was sick of the Italian family bullshit. Frankly, he was sick of being mean-spirited. He was sick of the phony turf wars. And he was sick of everyone killing everybody, and sick of watching his back. He could make it on what was left of Macro's million, but he thought, as Marilyn Monroe once said, that…*too much is not enough!* It was worth spending an effort to find the rest of the twenty million. It would take a lot of money to live the way he wanted to.

A month ago, Zio had met a blond named Padme, from some island in the Bahamas he'd never heard of, at the Tuscan Grill. She let him buy her a drink. She was waiting for friends. She was the most amazing female he had ever met in his life. He never thought a monster like him would meet an angel like her. She told him the secret of life: "What you put out there; you get back."

He was astounded at the revelation. In a heartbeat his life was changed: You shoot at someone; you get shot at back. You play nice, they play nice. You play rough, they play rough. You smile, you get a smile. You yell and scream, they yell and scream. Somebody is an asshole; he gets asshole back. Someone screws with you; you screw with them. You throw shit; it gets thrown back.

Padme had kissed him on the cheek and thanked him for the drink and he watched her leave with her girlfriends. He followed them, but his phone rang, and he was off to another crisis.

He realized that he was severely burned-out. He didn't wash his cheek where she kissed it for three days. He vowed to find her again. He was besotted.

He wanted out of the life of crime. Well, after one more crime maybe.

$ $ $

Zio paid a Mexican cab driver a thousand dollars to take the stripper he captured from the marina to Gator Park Airboat Tours on Alligator Alley west of Miami. He trusted the Mexicans more than he did his mob brothers. He thought that said it all. She was still blindfolded; she never saw his face. He had bought her a fanny pack, a pair of flip-flops, gym shorts, a windbreaker, and a T-shirt. He put twenty-five thousand in the fanny pack. What you put out there...[6]

$ $ $

Macro didn't fare as well. (Asshole; get asshole back.) The Japanese "disposal team" had a time of it getting him to keep his feet still while the concrete set. Finally, a hammer in the right spot did the trick. This cost Zio $5K;

---

6 She never went back to college. She never stripped again. She married a full-blooded Seminole who ran a family airboat excursion outfit for tourists in the Glades. They had five half-breeds—all girls. The whole family trapped alligators and snakes for zoos all over the world. They smuggled Caribbean girls into Florida through the Glades by airboat for domestic labor and childcare positions for the well-to-do. Some mother-son operation out of Haiti.

he had hired two local Japanese Yakuza branch soldiers to handle the details. A few days later, a group of recreational divers found Macro next to the Christ of the Deep statue in thirty feet of water off Key Largo. He had his arms up toward heaven, just like the statue.

Fish had eaten lots of stuff, like the nose, lips, eyelids, and so on. It was going to be a technical challenge to even discover the sex of the body. The county coroner just didn't have it in him that day to do a post/forensics/dental x-rays/stomach contents/and all the paperwork on just another hood making a statement for somebody—that wouldn't get identified anyway. Macro got a new alias: John Doe. After a year, if the body isn't claimed, the frozen carcass would be given to the medical school or the secret Army Ballistics Injury Testing Center on the Dry Tortugas.

$ $ $

Levi wasn't hard to spot. He was enjoying a club sandwich and a bucket of beers by the hotel pool. He had a nice view of the New River as it wound through downtown Fort Lauderdale and was enjoying watching the big white yachts passing by. Zio pulled up a chair and sat next to him, blocking Levi's sun. Levi, being wily, situationally aware, and avoidance-oriented, ran…confirming Guido's assumption that he was who he was looking for.

All pools in Florida are fenced (to keep kids from drowning?). Zio had zip-tied the only gate. He calmly walked up to Levi, who was desperately trying to rip the gate open, and put his arm around Levi's neck like they were drunken buddies. He whispered in his ear, "If you put calm out there, you will get calm back."

Levi found himself chained to the floor at the two-bedroom concrete slab house. He had shackles on his ankles chained to cuffs on his wrists. He had a dog electric training collar on his neck. Zio told him that if he so much as even coughed it would shock him with the power of a Taser. "You don't talk in your sleep, do you?" Zio teased him.

$ $ $

Guido in conversation with Zio: "You can have ten women a day if you want in Ecuador. Excellent wine and food at pennies on the dollar. Affordable recreational medications. Bribes are affordable. Affordable officials to bribe are plentiful. Everything is affordable."

They were brother-soldiers. It didn't matter who you worked for when you were a mercenary. You follow the money. Zio thought about Padme's rule of life: what you put out there, you get back. He explained all that to Guido. Guido allowed, as he would like to meet Padme too. He had major issues. Maybe she could give him a new direction too?

Zio said, "We split the money we have. Only not now. I don't trust you *that* much." They made a pledge to find the rest of the money if they could. They hoped it was still in Fort Lauderdale.

Cold beer came out. Zio uncuffed Guido.

Guido and Zio ended up taking a night off. They decided they would limit their drinking and tipping to just three thousand apiece. They didn't want to stand out. Zio gave Guido a wad of mixed bills. They were very popular with that as their budget even though it was really only a moderate amount for this type of evening's entertainment. They closed the club Pure Platinum and went home with a mother-daughter stripper tag team. It got pretty kinky. It cost another thousand. Zio and Macro agreed they got what they paid for.

The next morning Zio called a doctor who called in a prescription for Zithromax for both of them. Not Zio's first rodeo.

Guido woke up groaning, "I need a cold bowl of aspirin."

$ $ $

It was three the next afternoon before Guido checked his messages. They were all from one number. He quit listening to Popi's rants after number five. There were ten more he didn't bother with. Guido figured standing Popi up at the airport was a job breaker just by itself. He also figured that Popi had even less of an idea where the rest of the twenty million was than he did. At least now he had a contact with boots on the ground in Fort Lauderdale. Popi had nothing. And he would never find Levi.

Nursing lattes sweetened with Cuban rum, Guido said to Zio, "I know whose money it is, how much there is, where it was last seen, but I don't know where it is. I know that it was supposed to go to Bimini, and then Cuba, on a fishing boat named the *Master Baiter*." (Zio had a mouthful of hot coffee that he sprayed all over himself laughing.)

"That is why I was sent to Fort Lauderdale. Well, me and Levi. Maybe, between you and me, we can find it. I'm not sure Ecuador should end up being our retirement home though. We might have to find someplace else."

Zio: "The money belongs to an Ecuadorian. Yes, that could be awkward. I've heard great things about the Philippines. It is a rich country with many rich older women."

Guido: "It's even worse than that. The Ecuadorian works for the Chicago Mob. Part of the Black Hand. My boss's organization was supposed to retrieve the money in Cuba, and then start its laundering process in Tobago."

Zio: "I work for the Black Hand. Well, not directly. I work for a Mafia boss who is associated with the Black Hand. It's all a need-to-know secret society thing. I really don't know shit. I'm not even sure who I work for. So many layers. Mergers."

Guido: "We are just soldiers. Privates at that."

Zio: "This may work to our advantage. Their right hand doesn't trust the left hand. The right hand is jerking off, and the left hand has its thumb up its ass, then someone yells 'switch.' These guys shoot each other for looking at each other's girlfriend. Somebody is making a very loud statement by shooting a million dollars across a bow to make someone a fool, or as payment for a grudge, or to turn that bow into a giant lightning rod. Somebody is putting a wrench in a well-oiled machine. Confusion and suspicion. Blame and shame. We may be the only level heads in the game."

Guido: "And we are AWOL. They'll think we are involved."

Zio: "You can bet the feds are mobilizing too. This was a shot across their bow too."

Guido: "Let's buy a carwash with the money we got, in Australia. Go legit."

Zio: "Let's find Popi and have a chat with him. I say we stay in the game at least until things get so hot we have to bail."

Guido: "Popi will go to our condominium here in Fort L. Maybe he and us working together can pick up a trail to the money. That was what Levi and I were sent up here to do in the first place. Someone knows something at Lightningbolt Marina. Maybe that's where the boat with the twenty million left from. That's where we start."

Zio: "I need a partner. You need a partner. We screw with each other; we are no better off than the idiots we work for. I bought you the best lap dance of your life last night. That ought to count for something. Besides, if I screw with you, it will be after we get the money!"

Guido: "You're screwing with me already. Where's the million you took from me and Levi? And I assume the Bentley is already on a container ship."

Zio: "I gotta have some control over you."

Guido: "You already do. I'm homeless."

Zio said, "We'll get the money when we need it. Right now, what you don't know won't hurt you."

11

Padme called Coleman from Fort Lauderdale. "Get on the internet and Google Channel Seven in Fort Ladeda. Search for 'New millionaire has party, now missing.'"

Coleman answered. "Already seen it. Love the shot of him dancing on the margarita truck roof. He's a pretty good dancer. I swear that was the Lambada."

Padme: "I guess he disappeared after that."

Coleman: "Probably at the ER? That had to be a pretty good fall off the roof."

Padme: "Bet whoever is missing the money is looking for him. Bet there's gonna be more news about him. Hey, why don't you and Endi hop on the cruiser and join the party here. There is an empty slip at my condo. I'm getting kind of randy. Gimme Endi." Coleman handed the phone to Endi slowly shaking his head.

Endi: "What are you wearing?"

Padme: "Not much. You?"

Endi felt his urethra spasm. "Bathing suit."

Padme: "I bought a new set of panties and bra. Let me describe them to you. I'm standing in front of a mirror. The panties are kind of an Easter yellow. My wax lady did her best again. The bra, of course, is the same material, and my nipples are perking up just thinking of you. The bra is French, so it is pushing my tits together and lifting them. If I bend over at the waist, you can see nipples."

Endi: "Stop."

Padme dropped her voice to husky: "I have high heels on too. They require constant balance from the upper thigh, causing the muscles from the backside to tense and appear pert and ready for mating. They also tilt my hips, thrusting my ass up and out, as a provocation for the mounting by the male. But unlike most mammals, I am engineered to mate from both fore and aft."

Silence.

Padme: "You there, big fella?"

Endi: "I'm coming."

Padme: "As in actually, or actually?"

Endi: "As in I'm actually headed to Fort Lauderdale."

Padme: "Can you bring a mattress?"

They hung up and Coleman said, "I assume we are taking a mattress or two to Fort Lauderdale."

12

"How come he is standing in that five-gallon bucket?" Levi asked. Zio was showing him a picture on his iPhone of Macro Salsa forlornly standing in concrete.

"Because he can't get out," Zio answered as he waved a battery-powered nail gun around.

Levi: "Why can't he get out? What are you doing with a nail gun?"

"Because he let the concrete set around his feet." Zio fired a double tap. Two nails embedded themselves close to Levi's bare feet. Levi screamed and the dog-training shock collar around his neck went off. He screamed again.

Startled, Zio pulled the trigger on the nail gun again… accidentally. "Hey, sorry about that. You know if these things got a safety?" Zio waved the nail gun around looking for a safety. "You can talk. You just can't scream. I have the collar set for scream."

Levi: "Don't point that thing at me, ok? Can we speak Spanish for chrissake? I don't do English that well. Can you turn this collar off? Jesus! Why are you showing me that asshole from the marina standing in a bucket of concrete? Where's the million me and Guido took off that prick?"

Zio: "Si." He switched to Spanish. "The actual reason why this gentleman is standing in a pail of concrete is to test his upper-body strength. It takes strength to tread water with the extra weight of five gallons of concrete attached to your feet. You have to use your arms really fast. He failed the test. You look up to it though. So, where is Popi?" Zio squeezed Levi's biceps a couple of times. "Good muscle."

Levi answered with an attitude: "In Ecuador; if you're talking about my father-in-law, who by the way is connected, and is very, very pissed about you taking his money. And keep your fucking hands off me. Someone stole twenty million from him and that is why he sent me up here to find your ass and…ahhhhhh…shhhhhhiiiiit!" Zio hit the shock-collar remote he held in his hand.

Zio: "I am aware of all that. I'm just here to help. It's the right thing to do. I just want to be known for doing the right thing. When I get a chance to visit with Popi, maybe over a nice cold beer, I'm sure it will brighten his day knowing that you and I have cooperated together and have been doing everything in our power to get that money back for him." Zio fired another salvo of nails onto the floor. Levi screamed with his mouth closed. The shock collar went off anyway.

Zio: "Your father-in-law is pissed at you right now. He doesn't even know I exist, so how could he be pissed at me? In order to de-piss him, we have to find him first of course so…we can all get our heads together, and quit screwing around, and find the money. I feel that him loving and missing his son-in-law like he surely does, that he will be grateful to have you back and generously share the money, especially if I help him find it. It's a win-win-win. Give me your best guess as to where he might go when coming to Fort Lauderdale. We both know he is not in Ecuador." He fired one shot and a nail embedded itself in Levi's bare foot, stapling it to the wooden floor.

Screaming. Collar zap. Rage. Zap. More screaming. Zap. Zap.

Zio had decided to leave Guido out of the proceedings. "You know a Guido?" Zio asked Levi, nonchalantly examining a cuticle.

Defiance; silence.

Poof went the nail gun again. Screaming. More screaming. Spanglish cursing.

Zio: "Guido told us about you and your mission here in southern Florida."

"Stop with the nails. I'm cooperating the best I can."

Zio: "You are absolutely right. I am being mean-spirited. My guru and I have been working on that. Let me see if I have a Band-Aid. Does this hurt?" Zio poked the foot with the nail gun that had the nail in it.

"Goddammittfuckkingcocksuckercuntlickingdickbreathassfuckingholejesuschristonacrutch that hurt!!!!!" Levi did know cursing in English fluently, but he didn't know what most of the words meant.

Zio: "We got all we could out of Guido. He's not with us anymore. He told us Popi would be on his way to Fort Lauderdale or was already here. There is supposed to be a condo somewhere? Guido's parents should have sprung for swimming lessons by the way. And he should have worked out more at the gym tuning up that upper body strength. He sank very fast. The bigger you are, the harder you sink. So, it is time to tell me your lead that you were to pursue to find Popi's missing money, and where do we find Popi when he visits Fort Lauderdale?"

"Don't shoot that thing again."

"Sure thing. Now what is Popi's cell phone number?" Zio had his phone in his hand.

Levi: "I have no idea. It was in my cell phone. I left it at the pool as I was being kidnapped by you, ass… Aaaayeeeeeeeee!"

Zio: "Watch that attitude, Levi."

Levi: "Ok, ok. We have a condo here. I'll take you to it if you let me go. Popi is probably going there or is already there. I don't know the address; I just know how to get there."

Zio: "And so, if the family has a condo, why were you staying at a hotel, pray tell?"

"Because I rock-starred the condo the last time I was in this fucking town and Popi won't let me stay there ever again. Alright? Fuck you. I can't believe you killed Guido."

Zio: "It was an accidental drowning. Could have been avoided. Tragic loss of a precious life. God works in mysterious ways."

Levi: "You mind un-nailing my foot? I need some ointment. I'm allergic to Neosporin. You got any mupirocin? I don't want an infection. And I need a fucking bottle of Tylenol."

Zio: "You haven't told me about the lead Popi sent you with, that you were following. Like who do you guys think stole your money? How about we just pour some vodka over it? We'll let you soak it in the toilet first."

"All I know is that the boat with twenty million was supposed to have left from some marina called Lightningbolt. I don't know. We were just driving by and heard the mariachis. We grabbed the manager. He was our only lead. And you stupid fuck sunk him in the ocean. He probably has the whole twenty mil. Or had. I had some notes in the car too. Where's the Bentley, dill weed?"

Zio showed Levi another picture of the gloomy Macro Salsa in his Speedos standing in his five-gallon plastic bucket, between two grinning Orientals wearing giant dark glasses and ball caps hiding half their faces. They had their arms around Macro's shoulders. The Orientals looked exactly the same. And exactly the same as eight hundred million other Orientals in dark glasses and ball caps. They were waving at the camera. (Macro wasn't because his arms were tied behind his back.)

Levi: "Why are they smiling and waving? Looks like they have the twenty million."

Zio: "I really don't know. Maybe it's something Macro said. That Macro was such a clown. Hilarious. I assure you they aren't in it for the twenty mil."

Guido was in the next room listening to Zio interrogate Levi. Zio left Levi nailed to the floor and consulted with Guido.

Guido: "Not nice the crack about my parents not giving me swimming lessons."

Zio: "Sorry about bad-mouthing your parents. I just can't shake this cynicism I'm cursed with. I just can't help saying hurtful things. You said Levi was stupid, but I didn't believe you. He probably doesn't remember to wipe his ass. Why the hell did Popi send this shit-for-brains to Florida on this mission? He had to know it was going to be damn dangerous."

Guido: "I think Levi has a big dick. Popi's daughter started walking bowlegged day one after he showed up. I think it was worth it to Popi either way. If we found the twenty million, fine. If Levi got whacked, it was worth the twenty. A win either way. Where is the Bentley? Levi really did leave some notes in it."

Zio: "The Bentley is sealed in a container."

Guido: "I knew it."

Zio: "Never mind. We need to find Levi's daddy-in-law Popi now."

Guido: "I'm just giving you shit. I don't know who my parents were anyway."

Zio: "I'll go pull the nails out of his foot. Don't talk around Levi. I'll put a pillowcase over his head. Makes sense for you to remain dead for now. Feel free to punch him randomly if you want. You know, so he knows it's not just me guiding him through life. He says he will take me to Popi's condo here in Fort L. You know where it is?"

"Nope. Hell, this is the first time I've ever been to Lauderdale."

There was screaming with the nail removal process.

They loaded Levi in Zio's black Tahoe. Guido dropped Levi on his head twice. Spanglish, zap, zap. Guido stifled laughs. They propped him up in the front seat and zip-tied his neck to the headrest. Guido curled up on the rear deck of the SUV out of sight and nodded off, still drained from the mother-daughter stripper tag team the night before.

No one was at Popi's condo on the fourth floor of a massive condo complex. They stripped Levi naked and locked him in the master bathroom. They locked the bathroom door with a hasp and lock they installed on the outside of the door so he couldn't get out. They zip-tied his wrists behind him and his ankles together. They left the bark shock collar on. They chained his feet to the toilet and his hands to the sink's drainpipe. Zio took Levi's hood off. He put a gag in Levi's mouth.

They put a motion sensor in the living room. If anybody triggered it a pager on Zio's belt would go off.

There was nothing to do but wait and hope Popi, or somebody from the organization in Ecuador, would show up at the condo.

The condo was on the fourth floor. They figured no one would be coming through the sliding glass door on the deck. They made sure it was locked anyway.

They installed a lock on the condo's entry door that locked in whoever came in, trapping them. No one else, except Guido, could get in without breaking the door down.

Thus, carefully prepared, Zio and Guido resumed their titty-bar campaign. They had long ago learned patience and how to cope with long periods of boredom. Zio gave Guido another couple of thousand. They did their own thing this time, agreeing that the mother-daughter four-some thing had been a little disturbing. Besides, this time, they tried not to get lying-down, seizing, blacked-out drugged and drunk like they did last time. After all, they were on duty this time.

$ $ $

Guido's pager went off while a two-hundred-pound coal-black Nigerian woman with mammary glands the size of a Holstein's sat on his head and sucked his dick. He didn't hear the pager. He couldn't hear anything, much less breathe.

After he was finished, Ayeola Omodesireoluwa Nwanneamaka nimbly, for her size, dismounted and informed him that his pager had gone off during the servicing and that it would be one thousand dollars please and thank you and would you like a warm damp towel and could I get you something to drink? Some fruit? An ecstasy tablet? She had powdered herself down there with cocaine. In Florida, it's the details and courtesies that are so important to high-end specialty-service customers.

13

It was one in the morning.

By the time they got to Popi's condo, the Broward County Sheriff's Department (three cruisers and a SWAT team), multiple units of the Fort Lauderdale Police, an ambulance, and three fire trucks were randomly parked just as they had arrived, lights flashing, firefighters standing around, and officious police officers everywhere. There was yellow police barrier tape cordoning off multiple areas of crisscrossed confusion. A TV crew, forty-foot antenna mast deployed and generator humming, was camped out for the duration.

Zio and Guido joined the gathering crowd of onlookers. No one had a clue what was happening. A perky Hispanic reporter was a foot from a camera as big as her:

> *This is Adoration Candelabra Jose de Cuervodesa-Valderamerez live with KWHY-On-The-Scene-TV. As this critical hostage crisis continues, this reporter has just learned of the new bomb threat now made by the terrorists who have locked themselves in a condominium on the fourth floor of this building behind me. Our investigators have just found out that the condominium*

*is owned by a drug cartel in Ecuador. The police have
asked that everyone stay away. Please do not come
down to this scene as it may literally explode at any
time. It is estimated that the terrorists have enough
explosives to flatten the entire six-story condominium
behind me. The police are evacuating the whole building
as we speak.*

There was a second reporter translating what Adoration was saying into Spanish,[7] and a third signing for the hearing impaired, each with their own camera.

Portable floodlights illuminating the scene behind Adoration showed people streaming out of the condo building carrying cats, mothers, pitchers of margaritas, suitcases, huge pieces of horrible art, some leading tiny dogs, another a huge growling and lunging Rottweiler, in robes and underwear, in cutoffs and flip-flops, way over-weight, tattooed, canes, wheelchairs, crutches, walkers, yamakas, statues of Mary, and of course pictures and wall hangings of poor Jesus on the rugged cross. They were all pissed. They created a din.

Levi's noise had triggered a call from his neighbor below. That and the dripping water from the caller's ceiling that was under the bathroom that Levi was tearing up. The neighbor met the cops at the front door of the condo building and informed them that it was a hostage standoff by terrorists with a bomb. The neighbor was on his fourth day straight of celebrating his increase in disability for

---

7 Talk about irony.

PTSD to seventy percent. He had been a company clerk for a rear echelon supply company in Kuwait, but having invested in a *DSM-IV* he had convinced a counselor for the Veterans Administration that he had fifteen out of eighteen symptoms for PTSD and so couldn't hold a job. He looked normal. Talked normal. Cops didn't know everything he said had been a fabrication for twelve years. The cops had no alternative but to believe him because if they didn't and the place blew up, how would that look?

Guido and Zio watched a bomb-squad truck slowly parting the crowd. There was cheering and applause as a heavily padded team of bomb experts guided a radio-controlled robot (with its name on it: Pull-My-Finger), that laboriously climbed the steps on eight tires to the condo building's front door.

Zio said to Guido, "I thought they used Haitians for that?"

Guido said, "Those are probably Haitians in the bomb suits. I say we get out of here. Take the money we got and run. I completely underestimated Levitra's ability to screw things up. Besides, Popi will be here any time now. He sees me; shit on fan."

Zio: "You think he will see you in a crowd of ten thousand buried under the rubble from a six-story condo explosion?"

Guido: "Very funny. Our chances of recovering the rest of the twenty mil is zero at this point."

Zio: "Not if we capture Popi and start all over again."

Guido: "You're not kidding, are you?"

Zio: "Some kind of wonderful trap we set for Popi, huh?"

Guido: "See those firefighters over there smoking behind the ambulance? They look about our size."

Zio: "The fat guys? I know what you're thinking, and I like it, sort of."

They loaded the unconscious firefighters, stripped to their underwear, gagged, and tied up, into the ambulance and drove it behind the condo. The cop posted fifty feet from the back door opened the police tape for them and didn't nod or make eye contact. He had his hand in a bag of Dunkin' Donuts. They backed up to the loading entrance. Dressed in full firefighter gear…hats, suits, respirators, and carrying axes, a Jaws of Life, and oxygen tanks…they grabbed a stretcher and ambled through the back-door entrance of the condo.

At the top of four flights of stairs, Guido moaned, "I gotta sit down. How the hell do firemen do it? Schlepping all this shit upstairs? Just to save some fat-ass useless POS who lit his mattress on fire with a cigarette. And we're not even fighting smoke, heat, and fire." Guido panted like a steam engine that had just started moving.

Zio: "I heard that if you let a fat-ass citizen catch fire, they are impossible to put out. Fat burning."

Guido: "What does that have to do with anything? Let them burn up, what I would do. These goddam fireman hats are heavy." He wiped the sweaty top of his head with his arm.

Zio: "Just saying, firemen want to get them out of the burning structure before they catch on fire and have to carry them out on fire. I heard the most dreaded worse thing a fireman fears is when he has to fireman's-carry a big-assed, fat, smoldering, sizzling one."

Guido's panting had slowed some: "Ok, let's go." They abandoned the ax, oxygen tanks, and jaws-of-life. Guido threw his hat on the pile of jettisoned equipment. They kept the respirators on, shielding their faces. Zio dragged the stretcher behind him. They stumbled to the condo and opened the door. No swat teams, bomb squad, or security. They had guessed right—the threat of a bomb had stopped everyone from getting anywhere near the condo.

Zio: "You don't think there really is a bomb?"

Guido: "Come on. It's just Levi tearing things up."

Zio: "Well, there is no law saying that two things can't be going on at the same time. Maybe Levitra knows about the bomb. That's why he is going crazy."

Guido: "You got a point. Wish I had a bomb. I'd just blow up his ass and the whole place with it."

The bathroom door was splintered through the middle. The toilet apparently had made the hole as most of it was still in the door. A soaked Levi was kicking the vanity sink viciously. He saw Zio and Guido. A stream of unintelligible Spanglish profanity echoed off the porcelain and tile. Levi was still chained to the plumbing, but he had managed to kick the toilet completely off its base and water was spurting to the ceiling, soaking the light fixture exhaust fan, causing it to crackle and blink on and off. The smell of ozone was pungent and strong. Water was coming from under the sink as well. There was standing water an inch deep.

Guido took off his respirator mask: "For chrissake, Levi. You realize you got the whole of Fort Lauderdale's police, fire, and media assets down in the parking lot?"

Zio: "All you had to do was wait for Popi and we would have let you go. We need your help. Not this. Dumb-ass."

Levi to Guido: "I thought you were dead, dick-face."

Guido: "Obviously news of my death was exaggerated."

Zio said to Levi: "Why can't people just cooperate for the greater good? We're just trying to find your money. Same as you." He kicked Levi in the ribs.

Levi, writhing on the floor: "You got a Percodan or something? Everything hurts. I can't believe you shot my foot with a nail gun and you expect me not to try to get away. What's with the fireman suits? Don't kick me ever again."

Zio: "Levi, get on this stretcher and shut up."

Levi: "Are you kidding me? I'm not going anywhere with you…"

Zio cracked him on the head with the broken toilet seat. They loaded the limp Levi onto the stretcher and strapped him on. They re-tied his hands behind him. They covered him with a blanket. They used the elevator instead of the stairs. The stairs were clogged with people who were obeying the don't-use-the-elevator-in-case-of-fire rules. They loaded the babbling Levi into the ambulance and eased out the service gate.

The two firefighters tied up in the back of the ambulance were awake, but smart enough not to panic. Levi was conscious again, yelling and screaming from the back of the ambulance.

Zio: "Just drive."

Guido: "Plan?"

Zio: "No. You?"

Guido: "We still don't have Popi. We just made negative progress. We have two hostages and a naked damaged Latino that probably needs medical attention. The three have no value whatsoever. They are a liability, in fact. What the hell are we going to do with them? Jesus, what a pain in the ass it is to get rid of folks. They don't burn. They don't sink. They don't deteriorate. Who knew when we got into this business? Where's a Jap mobster when you need one?"

Zio: "Let's drive around front and see if Popi has shown up."

Guido: "Oh sure. Fine idea. With balls-breath back there screaming and yelling? I don't know how many more blows to the head he can take."

Zio: "He can handle more. Drive around front like I said." Zio got out of the passenger seat and stumbled over the firefighters in the back of the ambulance and crow-barred a small safe open and found some injectable vials. He mixed Demerol with Valium and told Levi to turn over.

Eyes wide open.

Zio delivered the cocktail via anal sphincter without the needle and the blood-rich mucosa of the rectum absorbed it faster than if he had injected it into a muscle. Levi's head lolled and a beautiful smile flushed his face.

Zio checked the shock collar. He told Guido, "The little shit used up the battery. His neck has a hole in it."

$ $ $

Guido: "That's him. That's Popi. Looks like he has two bodyguards with him too."

Zio: "You mean the bald little guy between the two bald big guys? There?" He pointed toward a trio of dark-complex-ioned, obviously South American men in classic white Cuban shirts with embroidery on the front worn outside the pants. The little one was hopping and waving his arms in front of a cop. The cop was expressionless; this happened to him every day. He was a motorcycle cop, in dark wraparounds (even though it was night), helmet, jodhpurs, and knee-high boots.

Popi bumped chests with the cop. The bodyguards closed in. The cop nailed Popi on the kneecap with his baton. He caught bodyguard one on the chin with the backswing from the kneecap strike, and simultaneously Tasered bodyguard two. Popi went to one knee screaming. Bodyguard one was also on his knees holding his blood-dripping mouth, and bodyguard two was on the tarmac seizing. The motorcycle cop sprayed all three with mace and they flopped around. The cop was thinking, *they're not supposed to seize like that…maybe the pepper spray is conflicting with some drugs?* Not his first rodeo.

Zio and Guido looked at each other. They drove the ambulance to the officer who now was zip-tying the three downed South Americans' hands behind their backs. "Want us to take these clowns to the hospital?" Zio asked the cop.

"That would be a nice gesture by an otherwise worthless fire department. Let me get you a cruiser escort."

"We don't need one. We already have a load of injured looters and we're heading to General. We radioed ahead that we need security when we get there. We already have an escort. We'll lock them in the back with the others. We should zip their ankles, don't you think, partner?" Guido nodded.

$ $ $

Guido: "Jeeze, now what? So…our progress is so outstanding that we now have half-a-dozen liabilities, instead of just three, in a stolen ambulance. That cop needs to go to charm school."

Zio: "I'm working on the fly here. We got Popi. That's all that matters. All cops are arrogant pricks—especially a motorcycle cop. At least he made it easy to grab Popi." There was thumping and muffled yelling from the back of the ambulance. Zio had closed the door between the back and the cab of the ambulance. Guido was driving.

Zio looked though the little window to the back of the ambulance and saw the bodyguards, their eyes dripping and still partially blinded from the mace, trying to jump up and down on the firemen. Everybody except Levi was yelling and screaming. Levi wasn't feeling anything thanks to his enema. One fireman was rolling like an alligator trying to avoid the pummeling. The other bit the ankles of his still-blind bodyguard attacker. Popi was on his back, kicking Levitra with his wingtips anywhere he could make contact. His eyes were also half closed and dripping from the pepper spray.

Zio, five minutes later: "They're beginning to tire." Guido had the lights flashing but had turned off the siren. He was driving along A1A enjoying the red lights and passing pulled-over cars. He slowed for drunken, stumbling, high-heeled, miniskirts, or bikinis.

Guido: "I could get used to this."

Zio: "Let's head for the Glades. I have a friend in the airboat tour business. He's good at making things you don't want disappear. Besides, the road trip will give us time to think. How's the gas?"

Guido: "We're full. I'm hungry." They parked the

rocking ambulance in the back corner of a Publix grocery store parking lot and grabbed beer, water, and some sandwiches and chips, used the bathroom, climbed back in the ambulance, stripped off their firefighter gear, and headed west, lights flashing, passing everything in sight.

Zio counted their money. He had fifty thousand plus on him. He considered stopping by the storage unit and getting the rest of the money, but figured he had plenty for now. Besides, they were in a hurry. When the fire department realized an ambulance was missing, he knew they better be scarce and no longer in possession of an ambulance. He knew where he could get cash for the ambulance 24/7. He closed his eyes and let Guido drive.

The back of the ambulance finally quieted down. Zio nodded off. Guido never had so much fun. Fireman for a day. Night turned to day.[8]

---

8 The ambulance became a taco truck in South Chicago. The sale of the equipment and lights paid for the conversion by the new owners. Win-win.

14

The crossing from the Bahamas to Fort Lauderdale turned ugly.

Endi and Coleman found themselves bobbing in the five-foot-long inflatable dingy. Its outboard had been stolen with the *Wet Spot*. At least they were left with the oars. They were drifting north with the current about as fast as they were rowing west.

They had been overtaken by a cigarette boat driven by two guys in Nixon masks who fired a shotgun over their bow. Coleman had gone below for his 38 Special shark-killer always kept on the boat, but it was rusted too badly to fire back at the twin Nixons. As soon as the cigarette boat came alongside, Coleman and Endi smelled heavy weed.

A Nixon shouted: "Dudes, we're pirates. We're taking your boat." Nixon 1 stumbled as he shouted the orders and dropped the shotgun he was holding (flip-flop fail). Nixon 2 laughed but had another shotgun still well in hand. Nixon 1 threw a line to Endi, who intentionally dropped it four times before Nixon 2 got ballistic (literally) and shot out one of the Chris-Craft's front windows.

Coleman shouted above the sound of his two engines

and their two engines: "I'll give you a mattress and a million dollars if you go away."

"Oh, right on, moron. Coming aboard." A Nixon fell onto the Chris-Craft and knocked the wind out of himself but didn't let go of the shotgun, which he had pointed right at Coleman's balls while he gasped for breath. His Nixon mask fell off. He put it back on, apparently hoping it was the same as dropped food—the five-second rule—if you put it back on really quick it was like it didn't happen.

For a moment he couldn't see because the mask was on upside down, and with the shortness of breath, not to mention the pitching/rocking deck, he fell down the steps into the cabin.

Coleman and Endi's merriment didn't help their case. Nixon boiled out from below almost as fast as he had fallen in.

It was over as fast as it had started. A Nixon commanded Endi and Coleman to take the motor off the dinghy, which they reluctantly did. It only took two more shotgun blasts in the air to get that accomplished. After that, Coleman and Endi resigned themselves to being the picture of acquiescence and cooperation. In return they negotiated successfully for water, their baseball caps, dark glasses, their wallets (empty of cash), ChapStick, sunblock, and a fresh bottle of Mount Gay rum. Endi had already pocketed a handheld GPS and his cell phone at the first sign of trouble. It wasn't his first rodeo.

Both Endi and Coleman, without talking to each other, had considered and rejected the idea of telling the pirates about the two million in cash hidden in the mattress. They both came to the conclusion on their own that that would be a game changer to their disadvantage. Inject a lot of money into a high-seas boat hijacking would result in you becoming chum. Just give them the boat, maybe they will stay thieves and not become murderers. Besides, so what? Maybe the Nixons would find the money, which would lead to probably hysterical unintended consequences.

The last they saw of *Wet Spot* was a Nixon driving and waving and toasting them with a long-neck Corona. Coleman's cruiser and the fire-engine-red cigarette boat disappeared over the horizon toward Florida in less than a minute. The castaways saw the cigarette/pirate ship's name on the stern painted in gold: *Eat Drink Don't Marry.*

$ $ $

Endi: "I kind of liked those guys."

Coleman: "You know, sometimes you just have to sit back and watch our mirthful God at work; He has got to have a sense of humor. It's possible that we couldn't have found a better way to spend a couple of million."

Endi: "Someone will take it from them. Oh, the excitement we will have caused. I give you a dollar, you spend the dollar, the next guy spends the dollar, and the next. I love commerce."

Coleman: "Drink?" He passed the bottle of rum to Endi, who took a healthy slug. He looked at the GPS. "We are pretty close to Florida. Maybe only another forty-five minutes…at fifteen knots. With the northerly trades drift and our rowing ability, I'm thinking we are making about one-point-five knots west. We could be there in five or six hours if we don't stop to catch our breath."

Endi resumed rowing. "Did you catch the weather for tonight? This is the Bermuda Triangle you know."

Coleman: "I only checked the weather *until* tonight. I assumed we would be in Fort Ladeda by tonight."

Endi: "No blame. Got cell phone reception yet?"

Coleman: "Nope. Row harder."

$ $ $

They got lucky, if you can call anything lucky while being in a five-foot inflatable boat (one shark bite and…) in the Atlantic. Luckily, the wind picked up from the east and began pushing them west. Plus, Endi reached Padme by cell phone.

They were at the Lighthouse Point Marina by seven thirty that evening, where they enjoyed conch fritters, crab cakes, and a couple dozen raw oysters at the Nauti Dawg Marina Café…on the water.

Padme had met them two miles out in a center-console twin-outboard thirty-three-footer. She towed the empty dinghy while the survivors revived themselves from their ordeal from a cooler of cold beer and a variety of dips and crackers. She made them take a vitamin C tablet in case they had caught scurvy.

15

The Nixons were face-to-face with Boner Bonadonna, owner of Lightningbolt Marina and Lounge.

"This is a piece of shit." Boner jumped up and down on the back deck of Coleman's cruiser. He threw the outboard motor in the water. "They don't even make Chris-Crafts anymore." Boner kicked the gunnel crying out in pain. He'd forgotten he'd taken off his Top-Siders. Since Macro Salsa had quit (disappeared), Lightningbolt had become the Temple of Doom. Without the service manager, no one knew the Mexicans' names, for instance; and the gross had plummeted. No one could find anything to do.

Boner finally stood silently appearing to be listening intently to the pirates plead their case. Heat waves emanated from his red-flushed head even in the 93-degree Florida heat.

Jason (Surfer Nixon—long, stringy, dirty-blond hair) and Shawn (Druggie Nixon—long black dreads) looked at each other. Both were thinking about just running.

"Mr. Bonadonna, it was the only boat we found. We'd been looking all day and were running short of gas. That thing of yours burns a million gallons an hour." Jason looked pitifully at the long red cigarette boat *Eat Drink Don't Marry* in the next slip, knowing he had just nose-dived from the edge of an extremely outstanding day to a staggeringly horrible day. He didn't exactly know how much trouble they were in, but he knew that with Boner Bonadonna, even a little trouble could have a lot of depth to it.

Shawn slurred (a little hashish on board to calm himself) brightly, "Since it's a piece of shit, nobody is going to be looking for it. Can we have it?" That was the wrong thing to say. Fire came out of Boner's every hole. He even pissed fire. The very ground he stood on caught fire.

"Youdumbsonsabitchescouldn'tfindyourassinaroomofassholesblowingmarijuanahitsinyourfacenowgoddamittakethispieceofshitoutowhereyoufounditandopenaseacockandsinkthemotherfucker…" He breathed deeply and resumed spitting burning splenic vitriol, "Get the fuck out of my sight now and take that goddam mattress with you…and take the next flight to Oz…and don't forget Toto…and the horse you fucking rode in on…"

"Boss, phone call." His dock manager, another Jesus from Mexico, had quietly come up behind Boner not wanting to startle Boss-Dios. Boner jumped straight up and hit his head on the *Wet Spot*'s Bimini frame, dropping him to the deck. Dazed, he could only point his unfocused eyes in the general direction of Blurry Jesus.

Jesus said, "Is de Porta Authorityies policesa forces. Dey wanta to knowing should you have seena a Christ Craft boat sooner or later nameded *Wet Spot*? And a grande red speed-a-boat named *Ead, Drin, Donna Marrrry*. And since you stand on de *Wet Spot* I thin maybe you shoulda taking call for you self." Jesus held out a portable phone.

Boner tackled Jesus and the two flew off the dock into the oily marina water, but not until they both had made contact with the rigidly thick hull of the red cigarette boat on the other side of the dock walkway. The phone went up in the air in a gentle arch and Shawn miraculously caught it like a basketball perfectly thrown from mid-court for a basket. Someone on the other end of the line squeaked demands. He put it up to his ear. "Uh, hello?"

"Whoever this is, we have it on good authority that you are harboring a vessel by the name of *Wet Spot* that was hijacked yesterday on the open seas by a cigarette boat named *Don't Get Married*. Drugs are involved. Our information points toward your marina. We are sending a team of investigators to investigate this investigation. Are you there? Is this Mr. Bonadonna?"

"No," answered Shawn innocently.

"And to whom am I speaking?"

"Shawn."

"Shawn the fucking who?"

"Shawn as in fuck-you-I'm-leaving." Shawn threw the phone in the water. Without asking why, Jason caught up with Shawn as they made a neck and neck Olympic-winning sprint to their ancient green (they had rattle-can painted it themselves) Saturn four door which, if it couldn't do anything else well, always started the first turn of the key. They backed into the car behind them (not the first time that had happened). They got stopped, still in first gear, at the electric gate. They didn't know the code.

Two black Ford Crown Victorias with dark tinted windows all around pulled up at the same time to the outside of the gate. Two suits/sunglasses got out and rattled the gate as if that somehow would make it open.

The Saturn died. Errrrr…Errrrr…Errrrr…it wouldn't start. Stringy and Dreads bolted back toward the boats. The Suits didn't get a look at their faces for all the hair, dark glasses, and ball caps.

Shawn and Jason, giddy and laughing, Nixon masks back on, loaded the mattress and the cooler with the remaining beer onto the cigarette boat, fired it up, backed into another boat (of course), and rocketed out of the marina into the ICW, throwing a tsunami left and right behind them rocking every boat in the marina causing a cacophony of threats and curses.

Paralyzed from exhaustion and out of breath, Jesus and Boner watched the Nixons stealing the boat. They were sitting in water up to their waists on the boat launch ramp. The ramp was covered with moss. Jesus started sliding. He grabbed Boner (neither could swim of course) and the two of them slid into the dirty water up to their necks, Jesus holding onto Boner's neck. The backwash from the big red cigarette boat had started their slide. They clawed their way back up the ramp, this time making it all the way out of the water. (It would have been funny if it hadn't been nearly fatal. Ok, it was funny.)

The marina was quiet for a moment except for the electric gate rattling. Even that stopped, the Suits finally figuring out that rattling it even all together still wouldn't open the gate. The cigarette boat's roar could barely be heard down the Intracoastal. Boner, lying on his back, closed his eyes: *I can't believe that POS Chris-Craft is back in my life. We should have kept it sunk when we had the chance after my nephew put two holes in its ass with the forklift. I wonder if the restraining order against Coleman is still in effect. Of all the goddam boats to steal…*

Jesus limp-skipped as fast as he could to a jabbering gathering of Mexicans ramping up for disappearance. The sight of two Crown Vics at the front gate called for evaporation into thin air. Fifteen Mexicans were over a six-foot fence and across the adjoining railroad tracks in fifteen heartbeats.

$ $ $

"Just let me up. I'll explain. I'm the victim here. I don't know what you're talking about. For shit sakes, take your goddam foot off my neck. Listen, you pricks, I'm gonna open a can of whoop-ass on your shit-for-brains dick-faces if you don't let me up." Boner was flat on his stomach, hands handcuffed behind his back, with a Suit's foot on his neck. He had not gone down without a fight. While he was fighting, he realized he was playing it all wrong.

"Ok, ok, I didn't have anything to do with this. Those dipshits that just stole my boat. They're the ones you should be after. They came in here with that stolen piece of shit old Chris-Craft trying to get me to buy it. I never saw them before in my life."

Suit took his foot off Boner's head. Boner stood up and kicked the Suit between the legs. He took off running. The Suits watched him with detached disinterest skid to a stop on his face after tripping over his own feet. (Except for the Suit with the red face holding his balls, who croaked out a feeble cheer.)

"I'm not kidding. I'm the victim here. Let me up. I gotta go try to get my boat back. You know how much that cigarette boat is worth. Hell, the gas she's carrying alone is worth thousands. It's a goddam tanker. Come on guys…toss me a bone here…I didn't do nothing…I'm just an honest businessman trying to make a…"

$ $ $

Pinky Blitz posted bail. "You need to see a doctor, Boner. You look like shit."

"You ought to see me from this side."

"You know, Boner, you need to quit kicking police officers. That is a habit you need to break. The seed you sew…"

Boner: "Fuck you. Just get me back to the goddam marina. You got the boys looking for my boat?"

Pinky: "It's already back home. We found it tied up at the Carnival dock. They said a cruise ship had just left. The *Carnival Ecstasy*. The two assholes that took your boat somehow managed to worm their way on board for the cruise. A guy at the dock said that two raggedy-assed junkie types tipped him a thousand to let them tie the cigarette boat to the dock and they bribed another guy to let them into the boarding area. The dock guy insisted that the junkie-types said that he could have your boat. He's quite sure now that he doesn't have a claim on it of course."

Boner: "Those two idiots never had a thousand at one time in their life."

Pinky: "Well, apparently they paid cash for the bridal suite with an outside private deck."

Boner: "Those fucks probably cashed in another boat they hijacked, then went out and got that POS Chris-Craft and tried to get me to believe that's all they got that day."

Pinky: "That would mean they are not as dumb as they look, which I find very hard to believe."

Boner: "And they are now in international water enjoying single malts and killer buffets on my dime. When does that cruise boat get back?"

Pinky: "Who knows? Maybe they will fall off. They probably will get off in Tortuga and miss the boat and stay wherever they got off. Let it go, Boner. We got your boat back. The port authority said they had no reason to arrest the idiots based on your hearsay. And they let you go. You don't even have to show up for the assault charges on the port authority officer. They know you didn't steal the Chris-Craft either."

Boner: "What? People just show up with cash and get on a cruise?"

Pinky: "Happens all the time they say. Rich folks do rich folk things. They left a ripped-up mattress on the *Don't Marry.* I had my boys throw it away when they got the boat back to Lightningbolt. And a beat-up old cooler and a couple of Nixon masks. No idea what's with the masks?"

Boner: "When do they let us retire, Pinky? Or are we just going to be unceremoniously offed when we're no use to them anymore, because if Chicago is just going to sink me with some concrete blocks, do it now. I can't go on like this anymore. Where are all my Mexicans?"

Pinky: "Oh, come on, Boner, it can only get better. This is just a minor career skirmish. The Mexicans will wake up in the morning like a chicken…with a blank slate. They always come back. Listen, by the way, this has been expensive. Bail was…"

Boner: "Why was the port authority there anyway? Who the fuck called them?"

Pinky: "They were looking for the Chris-Craft and the cigarette boat? Damn if I know why. I'm not on their need-to-know list. Who knows what those two assholes did while they were burning gas in your boat? What kind of stupid were you to let those two go play pirate?"

Boner: "I should have gone to beauty school."

16

The next day, Coleman and Endi sat in director's chairs on the back of *Wet Spot* enjoying the liveaboard life at Lightningbolt Marina and Lounge. They'd fished their outboard motor out of the water and hosed it off. It now lay between them on the back deck of the Chris-Craft. They'd made friends with the couple in the next slip, inviting them to visit Coleman's place sometime on Conch Key. The wife had a sister she wanted Coleman to meet. The husband wore a Jimmy Buffet T-shirt that on its back said: *The weather is here; wish you were beautiful.* Such was the boat community. Southern Florida was why they all put up with Southern Florida.

They had a blender going in the galley. They each held a crushed ice margarita in a traditional salted-rim stemmed glass. Coleman had opened a patio umbrella that he had rigged years ago to the transom for shade. They were plugged in, the AC was booming in the cabin, and two fans swept the deck with moist marina-smell salty air. Island music softly filtered through the din of the marina (the Mexicans were back) from built-in speakers on the Chris-Craft.

Padme was on her back on a large beach towel on the front deck in her yellow polka-dot bikini and a large floppy hat covering her head. Ohm was lying on his back next to her, sunning his genitals and occasionally licking them.

$$\$ \ \$ \ \$$$

The night before, Pinky had treated Boner to an evening at the mob-owned strip club to help "get his head back on straight." Boner had slept until noon, felt immensely better, snorted a small line of coke, drove the marina pickup through the entrance gate, pulled up to the service office, and saw Coleman and Endi. It was like a hot air balloon hitting a high voltage power line: sparks—deflation—explosion—basket plummeting to the ground—screams of rage and pain.

Coleman: "Hey, Boner. Thanks for finding my boat. Where'd you find it, anyway?"

Endi: "Nice cigarette boat." He nodded in the direction of *Eat Drink Don't Marry*. "Haven't we seen this cigarette boat before, Coleman?"

Boner: "You can cut the shit. Some assholes stole my boat and tried to sell me that piece of shit Chris-Craft you are sitting on that is occupying my slip, that is probably sinking right now not to mention polluting my marina."

Coleman: "And *Wet Spot* would be sinking because of where your asshole Macro Salsa, who hired your nephew, who put a hole in it with a forklift five years ago?"

Boner: "Macro quit. Haven't seen him. What you want anyway? It ain't free to take up one of my slips and plug your asses in like you own the place. I need two months' deposit. You have to pass the community restrictions, which you just failed. Get off my place. He glowered at Coleman: "I still have a restraining order against you, Coleman!"

Coleman: "I'm looking for my mattress. A Posturepedic. It's rather valuable to me. I've got quite a few notches on it, if you know what I mean." Wink, wink, elbow, elbow.

Boner: "It's in a dumpster at the cruise ship docks. It was all ripped up. Shrivel-dicks stole my cigarette boat again, apparently loaded the mattress, and somehow had enough money to book an on-the-spot cruise that was just leaving."

Endi looking at Coleman: "Questions answered. Shall we go, Captain Coleman?"

Coleman looking at Endi: "Let's shove us off." He shouted at Padme, "Better move your ass, sister…bus is leaving."

Boner: "That's it? What did I say that got you moving? I'd like to know. Nothing has ever worked with you two before."

The blowers came on. The umbrella came down. A minute later both Chevy V-8s were rumbling and bubbling exhaust underwater. Endi hopped out of the boat to untie her, bumping Boner who, with arms windmilling in a blur, fell into the water. He hit the cigarette boat on the way down, this time breaking an ankle, or at least it felt like it.

Lines cast off, Endi hopped on as Coleman idled the *Wet Spot* toward the Intracoastal barely making a ripple. Endi turned up the music and topped off everyone's drinks. People waved from other boats like happy boaters do. Padme clung to Endi like happy girls on boats do. Coleman blew his horn like happy captains do. Ohm was on the bow, nose into the wind, like happy boat dogs do.

$$\$ \ \$ \ \$$$

It seemed like the ambulance would never come. Boner cussed out the firemen/paramedics. "You shitheads took your time. What if I was dying, assholes? Gimme a pain shot."

Mexicans had circled him. They had answered his screams and pulled him out of the water. They were signaling each other about scattering again, assuming this would somehow be their fault.

The paramedic answered menacingly, "Then you would be dead and a hearse would be here, not me. Don't blame us. Some dicks stole one of our ambulances and kidnapped its crew and so we're shorthanded. Spread thin. How did you break an ankle falling off a dock? Jesus!"

Three Mexicans reflexively answered, "Si, Senor?"

Two others ran thinking they were being accused of stealing an ambulance. The rest took up the run for independence and followed the first two over the fence and across the tracks. (They see one run, they all run; ask why later.)

17

Zio and Guido bought an old Sebring cream-colored convertible for cash off a used car lot in Everglades City. Top down, they were listening to salsa, cruising the speed limit on Highway 29 north out of Everglades City toward I-75, the Everglades Parkway, and then back to Fort Lauderdale. They had left the firefighters in the ambulance, which had been taken to Naples. The firefighters were put aboard a container freighter headed for the Panama Canal and then onto points west.

The captain of the container ship had been told that under no circumstances were his new passengers to see the light of day until the freighter was on the open ocean. No telephone privileges. It had cost Zio only ten thousand dollars, plus Levi's passport (almost better than the cash), which he considered a bargain for getting rid of a couple of humans. He got that much for the ambulance. He gave each of the blindfolded firemen ten thousand in cash, one of Popi's credit cards, and a Popi bodyguard's passport.

Popi's bodyguards and Levitra went on an airboat tour of the Everglades. That cost another three thousand. (Extremely reasonable for disposing of three humans, they thought.) Quite a tour was promised. They were going to experience some things the average tourist doesn't get to. Guido wished them bon voyage and asked the tour guide if he had plenty of marshmallows for the alligators.

Popi was in the back seat of the convertible buckled in. Zio had tied a woman's big floppy straw hat on him and had treated him to a triple frozen strawberry margarita, an Ambien, and a Zoloft. He seemed content. The brim of the hat flapped in the wind, sometimes blinding him by covering his wraparounds. He didn't seem to notice. In fact, he didn't even move when a bird glanced off his head.

When Popi was asked by Guido whether he wanted Levitra to come with them or go on a tour of the Everglades with the bodyguards, Popi didn't hesitate: "Tour, tour, tour."

$ $ $

As they neared Fort Lauderdale, Popi became cognitive enough to explain to Zio and Guido that all he knew was that the boat left from Fort Lauderdale, and Ignacio, and the boat, and twenty million have not been heard from since. The boat was possibly sighted in Freeport, Bahamas, in a marina for one night. It was gone the next morning. Never seen again.

Guido to Zio: "He didn't know anything more than that when he sent me and his stupid son-in-law Levitra up here. I guess the trail stopped in the Bahamas."

Popi: "Well it didn't stop there. Show me the money. That idiot at the marina? Where did that million go? That's my money. Turn around."

Zio: "Off to the Bahamas we go."

Guido to Zio: "Popi will try to run. Or contact some more goons somehow. Do we really need him?"

Popi: "I heard that. Absolutely you need me. Only I know what Ignacio looks like."

Guido to Zio: "He's getting perky. He needs to be restrained. We need some rope."

Zio: "He doesn't even know what the boat looks like. He's probably never seen Ignacio either. We just sent the one person who maybe knows what Ignacio looks like into the Everglades."

Guido: "Are we ever going to get smart about all this shit?"

Zio: "And you wonder why we are just soldiers?"

Guido: "We should have sent Popi on the tour and kept Levitra."

They bought a dog chain and used it to tie Popi's wrists and ankles together.

$ $ $

The salsa music playing over the Sebring's radio was interrupted by a news flash:

This is your station for breaking news in greater southern Florida and the Keys…the voice of Miami… KWTF. And I'm Candelaria Lupe Andeladora DeJesus Zavarjelos-Smith.

It has been discovered that two men stole a valuable cigarette boat from a Fort Lauderdale Marina yesterday, only to abandon it soon after, then bribed multiple customs officials, cruise-line employees, and dockworkers in order to board the cruise ship Carnival Ecstasy *that was just about to sail from Fort Lauderdale for a ten-day Caribbean cruise. The two Caucasian males in their thirties are said to have paid cash for the bridal suite, purchased Rolexes and gold jewelry, bought a complete wardrobe in the ship's mall, visited the salon for haircuts and manicures, and lost twenty thousand dollars in the ship's casino before attention by ship security centered on their activities. It is alleged that the two suspects' inquiries as to the availability of illegal recreational drugs was the cause for Carnival security to investigate their activities.*

The newlywed couple, Chad and Coochie Schlongnight, made available the bridal suite for the pair of wealthy stowaways for twenty-five thousand in cash. When the new Mrs. Schlongnight was asked why she gave up her dream honeymoon suite, her comment was, "Duty-free, duh."

According to a reliable source on the Ecstasy, *close to two million dollars in cash was found hidden in their suite. The two stowaways are in custody and the ship is currently drifting in international water off Miami reportedly waiting for the arrival by helicopter of officials from the United States FBI and the IRS.*

$ $ $

Popi sat bolt upright when the word "million" came out of the car's speaker. "Ese es mi dinero, mutherfuckers! Turn around."

Padme sat bolt upright, knocking foreheads with her plastic surgeon. He was popping the capsules that formed every six months around the implants in her breasts. (She wasn't regular about doing her breast exercises.) Her iPod earbuds pulled out as she collided with the doctor. She was listening to salsa on KWTF, Miami.

"Sorry dear if I hurt you, sweetheart," the surgeon said with a lisp. He looked like a twenty-something perfect-specimen-Arian-breeding-stock-Nazi-Ken doll. He was in his fifties.

"Get out of my way. Watch my dog. I'll be back." Padme pushed him into his nurse (Barbie) as he rubbed his forehead. Padme ran topless out to her Mercedes, entered the driver's code, retrieved her cell phone, and leaned against the car. "Endi, answer the phone, you dildo." She had to try again before he answered.

"And to whom may I have the pleasure?" Endi answered, knowing it was Padme.

Padme: "Pleasure yourself, Stroker. You'll never guess what I heard on the radio just now."

She told him about the millions found on the cruise ship.

Endi: "We heard the same news flash. The plot sickens."

Padme: "Somehow they got my mattress, found the money, stole a cigarette boat, bought their way onto a cruise, and got caught. God, I love it! You guys are such fun. Must be the Nixons."

Endi: "Gotta be the Nixons. What a story. The FBI and the IRS? I think I'll call my friendly branch of whichever answers the phone first and offer a concerned citizen tip concerning one Lightningbolt Marina and Lounge, stolen boats, piracy, ad nauseam. What are you wearing?"

Padme: "Actually I'm leaning against my car in the parking lot of my boob-job-dude topless. I'm actually flattered. I've gotten some attention, which is unusual for Florida. People have become so desensitized to bare breasts these days you'd think we were in Africa." Endi overheard Padme talking to somebody, "Oh that's sweet of you to say. He did do a good job didn't he? Stands behind them too. They do take maintenance. Good luck, sweetie."

Endi: "An admirer?"

Padme: "Mother-daughter. Mom's taking her kid in for her first boob-job eval. Isn't that neat? I wished her good luck." With hands over her mouth and phone, Padme whispered, "Between you and me…not a pretty child…a regular Chelsea Clinton. Gonna be a long expensive rebuild before dad gets that one married off. He must be one ugly dude."

Endi: "All I got was braces."

Padme: "Toodle-oo. Go make your calls."

Ohm had both the doctor and the nurse in the corner. Teeth bared and a seethe with each exhale.

Padme lay back down on the treatment table. Ohm went back under the desk and licked his anal glands.

Padme: "Doctor, can you take out little Ohm's anal glands sometime? They are quite annoying."

$ $ $

Someone answered, "IRS."

"Tax evasion tip hotline please?" Endi asked.

"Please hold."

Coleman called the FBI at the same time Endi called

the IRS—a race. They bet a bottle of Moet & Chandon champagne and rib eyes at Ruth's Chris Steak House on who would take the shortest time to be able to talk to someone that had a clue or gave a shit.

They compared music on hold. It was the same. "That is very interesting," commented Endi.

Coleman got hung up on by the FBI. "Bet's off."

Endi said, "You know this is giving me the creeps… having anything to do with the IRS. I would seriously like to forever never be heard of by the IRS." Coleman appeared to be not listening, an earnest stare on his face.

Five minutes went by. The music had repeated itself four times.

"IRS Special Agent Joshua Tree." Endi almost dropped the phone.

Endi tried the blurt-it-all-out-at-once plan: "I want to report a money laundering scheme operation out of a Lightningbolt Marina and Lounge run by a Boner Bonadonna and Macro Salsa, who supposedly won a million dollars who sent his pirates in a red cigarette boat named *Eat Drink Don't Marry…*" He looked at Coleman, "A-hole hung up on me."

Coleman stood up doing his Rocky dance and shouted, "APPENDIX!"

$ $ $

Downtown Miami, eighth floor, the federal building: Joshua Tree: "Can you believe I just got off the phone with some scrotum that tried to tell me about a money laundering scheme with two pirates, a stolen red cigarette boat named *Eat Drink Be Merry*, or some such bullshit, and some guy at a marina called Thunder-prick named Boner…Salsa. Jeeze, and won a million dollars of drug money? What we have to put up with."

"I hear ya. You hear about those two guys that bribed their way onto a cruise ship in Fort Ladeda with a couple million in cash and abandoned a stolen red cigarette boat from a Lightningbolt…"

The two agents looked at each other as metaphysical light bulbs lit above their heads.

"Isn't that what we just sent Peabody to look into?"

"Yea, him and the FBI guy that's tagging along."

"You got that guy's number that just called on caller ID?

18

The helicopter made multiple passes trying to set down on the fantail of the *Carnival Ecstasy*. The wind was blowing twenty knots and gusting to thirty. The giant ship didn't slow down or turn into the wind, making it hard. The pilot even flew straight at the bridge hoping to get someone's attention. She swore there was no one up there.

The captain of the *Carnival Ecstasy* hadn't pointed the huge ship into the wind because no one told him a helicopter was trying to land on the fantail. In fact, he wasn't even on the bridge. He was asleep. It was three in the afternoon. Mostly his job was to sit at the captain's table and entertain passengers that paid extra to eat breakfast, lunch, or dinner at the captain's table. He was on board because every ship had to have a captain. In truth, the floating hotel just ambled along following a GPS program on its own. (The GPS and thrusters did a better job of docking the monster than he had ever done.) Sometimes he wouldn't go up to the bridge for days. He was expected to tan and work out. And compliment older female passengers. (To a table of eight female blisters in their seventies: "I know what it takes to sit at this table! You have to be young and pretty!" Titter, titter, hee, hee.)

The cruise ship's navigation computers overrode the command by the helmsman to stand to for incoming landing helicopter traffic. There was a schedule to keep.[9]

Normally helicopters don't care about crosswinds, but the pilot flared a little too early, with the nose up a little too high, just as a frivolous downdraft spilled from the huge ship's superstructure across the pool and down two flights of steps and right into the nose of the chopper. This happened just as the ship's stern sank twenty feet as a larger-than-usual swell passed on by. The little bubble canopy helicopter hit tail first, bouncing the tail rotor protector shroud off the deck causing the old H-13 Sioux helicopter, painted pink, to skid nose first into a deck chair that the on-hands-and-knees rent-a-cop had been sitting in moments before, watching the air show. He had a front-row seat. He didn't report the helicopter attempting to land because he figured the bridge knew. He'd never been allowed on the bridge anyway. In fact, he didn't know where it was.

"IRS," sitting in the center of the helicopter seat, pushed CIA out of the cockpit and leapt over him, fell to his hands and knees, and kissed the deck over and over like he was praying to Allah. He flipped over onto his back looking up at the blades of the helicopter still winding down. He crossed himself repeatedly, his lips moving unheard.

---

9 The ship was actually being controlled from a windowless room in the basement of corporate headquarters on NW 87th, Miami, Florida. The crew on the ship was just there in case all the GPS satellites fell to earth at the same time.

CIA stumbled over IRS, stepping on IRS's neck, and weaved toward the security guy who was trying to untangle his utility belt full of accessories from his M16 while trying to stand up.

CIA said to himself, *I cannot believe the fucking company couldn't get me a ride on a fucking decent helicopter for this fucking mission.*

The helicopter pilot, wearing smoky, tinted, pilot-style Ray-Bans, took off her flip-flops and put on cork high-heel sandals, tucked her pink blouse into her red Capri pants, undid a top button (it was hot on deck), pulled out her compact, powdered her nose, and refreshed her lipstick. She took her ball cap off, threw it into the helicopter, and her long thick blond hair fell over her shoulders as she shook it out. She took a large leather canvas overnight bag from behind the seat of the helicopter, looped its strap over a shoulder, and headed up the steps to the pool area, then beelined to the bar, perched herself on a stool, and ordered a Yellow Bird—tall, no fruit.

Hundreds of eyes, male and female, had followed her landing approach and her approach to the bar. The back of her shirt had the pink breast cancer symbol on it under the company name, Knockers Helicopter Charter.

After emptying half the drink in one suck of the straw, she lit a Player's unfiltered cigarette with gold Dunhill lighter.

"No smoking, mam," the bartender tried.

"I'm in the middle of the ocean, outside, and I just about sank this boat with a fire and brimstone helicopter crash because Captain Lot wouldn't slow down this bunker-fuel-burning-stink-pot floating Sodom and Gomorrah ocean liner, which I astoundingly managed to avert with pluck and talent, and you say I can't settle my nerves with a cigarette? Well, sodomize yourself and the horse you rode in on. Nice Yellow Bird, by the way." She raised the glass to him and sucked it empty. "Start me another." She looked toward the stern, half expecting her two passengers to have followed her up by now.

CIA's name was James Ian Fleming Bond. He vomited on the rent-a-cop who had mistakenly (he paid for this bad judgment instantly) cracked him on the nose with the butt of his (empty) M16. Bond (James Bond) disarmed the man, partially dislocating the man's elbow, and with a combat boot on the downed man's neck, pulled a zip-tie out of the side pocket of his black cargo pants, and tied the screaming man's wrists together. All faster than you can vomit twice, which he did this time on himself. He pulled a canteen from his web belt and swished his mouth, then spit it over the rail. Wind blew it back into his face. He slapped his holster for his Beretta. It was lying on the deck under the helicopter. He allowed, as the mission was not off to a good start.

Bond (James Bond) stumbled his way back to the helicopter, nose in the air due to the nosebleed, retrieved his gun, collapsed, leaned back on the helicopter, and rocked his head back pinching the top of his nose.

His partner's (IRS) name was Peabody. No one knew any of his other names. He was legally blind without his glasses. As he picked them up, he stepped on Bond's (James Bond) hand, whose other hand reflexively karate-chopped his crotch.

They both sat under the helicopter absorbed in their own little world of pain and nausea.

$ $ $

"Buy you a drink, Ms. Udder?" It was the ship's social director. "Not planning to fly back tonight?"

"Eight hours, bottle to throttle. I'd say not." She held up her empty glass to the bartender, who replaced it with a fresh one.

Social director to bartender: "This young lady's drink is on me."

Ms. Udder: "Dave, that's very chivalrous of you, but since all my drinks are FUCKING FREE on this floating zoo, as you know, go lick someone else's ass. Don't be sniffing around mine. Why would I want another asshole in my pants anyway? I already have one."

"I get off at midnight, Ms. Udder. Taco."

"Not this midnight."

$ $ $

A waiter called the infirmary, which hauled the rent-a-cop away. Then he led Bond (James Bond) and Peabody to the purser's desk whereupon the assistant purser led them to the makeshift jail that had been created in one of the dry goods lockers in the huge midship's galley where the Nixons were held.

Bond (James Bond) started interrogations.

Peabody followed the assistant purser to the business office suites where the head purser opened a safe and pointed to a stack of U.S. currency stuffed into one-gallon Ziploc bags.

Peabody started counting. (Counting money made him feel restored.)

$ $ $

"My name is Bond, James Bond. I'm a special agent with the Federal Bureau of Investigation." He stared at the Nixons, his eyes moving from one to the other slowly with a menacing expression on his face.

Squirming. Sweating. Looking at each other.

"We found it in a mattress."

"Bastards were going to kill us."

The Nixons couldn't wait to tell Bond (James Bond) everything.

He didn't believe a word they said—what with their haircuts (one—waves and streaking; the other neatly shaved bald), shiny fingernails, Rolexes, gold chains, large diamond pinky rings, Tommy Bahama everything, Tanino Crisci Lilian–style shoes, Thom Browne gold side-shield round sunglasses, and the results of a twelve-panel drug test (courtesy of the ship's human resources manager) that tested positive for cocaine, methamphetamine, marijuana, opiate, phencyclidine, ecstasy, barbiturate, buprenorphine, tricyclics, propoxyphene, and oxycodone, not to mention a breathalyzer count taken just before incarceration that read 0.191 and 0.184, respectively. Besides, they were laughing hysterically.

Jason: "Hey, we want something to eat…G-Man."

"You're in a giant food pantry, dumb shit. Have a

Cup-a-Soup. A bowl of cereal. Put some powdered milk on it. I don't want to see a mess in here in the morning."

Bond (James Bond) turned out the lights. There was screaming and pounding. He zip-tied the handle to the door of the locker so it couldn't be opened. He thought to himself, *you would think a resort like this would have a jail. A food pantry for a holding cell? Isn't there supposed to be a brig…?*

He decided to find a bar. He'd try again in the morning when they were a little more sober. He took their wallets for "evidence."

He hoped the hottie helicopter pilot hadn't seen him throw up. But she was only one of a thousand dishes on this floating eat-at-the-Y smorgasbord and hide-the-salami fest. She looked pretty hard to impress anyway.

He decided he would have one (maybe two) double Manhattans; then make a visit to duty-free for plumage. There was plenty of money in the boys' wallets. He decided no one, including the idiots whose wallets these were, probably knew how much they had, and no one would miss a little. Hey, the job was dangerous. It wasn't like he was buying a Rolex. He can't spy around the ship in black assault gear with puke on it even if he took off the shoulder holster and web belt. He had to blend in. *Why didn't his supervisor tell him to pack some cruise clothes?*

Jason and Shawn managed to get the lights back on (one of them brushed against the light switch next to the door during their panic). It didn't take long for them to find the sherry. They opened several bottles before they found one they could stand. They settled on an oloroso with nineteen percent alcohol. They enjoyed chips, trail mix, jerky, olives, and assorted chocolates with their wine.

$$\$ \ \$ \ \$$

The sous-chef for making toast opened the dry-goods locker at four thirty in the morning. He dreamily wondered why he had to cut a zip-tie locking the food pantry. If he hadn't been yawning so wide that his eyes were closed, he would have noticed that two guys were passed out on the floor just inside the door. He tripped and fell over the comatose Shawn, knocking himself dizzy on a fifty-five-gallon plastic drum of Spanish olives. By the time he could focus, the Nixons had bailed.

19

Padme: "There's a press conference I think we should attend. A city councilman needs bribing from a whore, or a stripper, and have it watched on the six o'clock news. He heads up the Development Commission. He's tearing down all the cool old places on the Fort Lauderdale canals and letting townhouse rows take over."

Coleman asked her, "Where did this come from out… of the blue?"

Padme: "This foreskin is on the board of directors of Select Comfort and a large stockholder. They make Sleep Number mattresses. They are always bad-mouthing us. And their mattresses suck. They get moldy, leak air, and then there is the trench effect. You gotta know about mattresses to understand."

Coleman: "So that's it; you want to screw him over because he is the competition?"

Padme: "Pretty much."

Endi: "What is the trench effect?"

Padme: "Ok, two sleepers have significantly different sleep numbers. The foam insert in the center of the bed will fail one way or the other toward the low number, and both partners then tend to roll toward the middle. Also, the mattresses leak, especially if the partners are three hundred pounders, or very active sexually. They are just glorified air mattresses. They tend to slow leak all night, you wake up on the deck, and then the next night you have to dial up the sleep number to keep the damn thing inflated through the night. Finally, the whole thing fails. Stilettos have been known to puncture them too."

Coleman: "We can't hose him just because he's the competition."

Endi: "Can too."

Padme: "The real reason is that he uses the right-of-eminent-domain thing and condemns small condos and hotels that have boat liveaboard docks on their water side. He is single-handedly obliterating 'old-Florida.' Some people that get kicked out have lived there on their boats for decades. They literally end up homeless. Zero compensation."

Coleman: "I really don't know any whores or strippers, although I have nothing against them. In fact…"

Padme: "This asshole councilman is hell-bent on destroying the liveaboard community in Fort Lauderdale, putting thousands out of their boat-homes and erasing a lifestyle that has been part of Florida since the '50s. I think it totally sucks. You can't tax the crap out of liveaboards like you can a condo owner. So naturally they want condos. You drive down one of the roads between the canals off Las Olas, and instead of neat old places with lines of sailboats and cruisers tied up out front and boat people having parties around the pool, you see high-rise condos. You can't even see the canals anymore."

Coleman: "What's his name?"

Padme: "Pinky Blitz. There is a ribbon cutting tomorrow at an old apartment/hotel, announcing the development of a new row of high-end condos. Tomorrow morning at eleven. There are already demonstrators camping out on the lawn of the place. It's called the Riviera. Pinky's grandfather founded the "Combine," which was the first gambling syndicate in the early twentieth century. So, Pinky was raised on the dark side from day one. He's also in the concrete business, so building new sea walls and condos means business. And he is a finger puppet for Chicago. He buries his enemies in concrete. He also puts people's feet in five-gallon buckets of concrete and drops them in the ocean."

Coleman: "Enough said. Let's do it. Only we don't have a million handy since the Nixons wiped us out."

Padme: "Here's the best part. He and Bonadonna are in business together. The Bonadonna that is the owner of Lightningbolt Marina. Boner Bonadonna."

Coleman: "The plot sickens. I wonder whatever happened to Macro Salsa?"

Padme: "We don't actually need the cash. The damage can just be done by the media."

Endi: "We gonna ask this Boner guy about Macro tomorrow at the news conference? See if he liked the mariachi band, the Marching Cobras, and the rodeo. You know that whole thing had to make him nervous."

Coleman: "Would not surprise me if Boner offed Macro and has the million. Yes, a press conference would be a great time to ask Boner a few awkward questions about Macro and the million.

Endi: "Which one of us wants to be a reporter tomorrow?"

Padme: "That would not be me. Fort Lauderdale is my stomping ground. That's why I suggested a stripper. That and for embarrassment's sake. Trashy stripper preferably."

Coleman: "Let's go to a strip club, make a selection, buy one, and then head to a trashy women's clothing store. How much do you think a stripper will cost, keeping in mind we will let her keep the outfit of course?"

Padme: "Depends if she is a single mother, for instance. Or is she trying to go to college? Or whether she just blows it on blow?"

$ $ $

Endi's cell phone rang. Ohm growled and snarled hysterically at the phone; he did it every time any cell phone rang. He wouldn't stop until the phone was held up to his mouth and he got to scream at it for a few seconds. It had started when Padme once downloaded a "dog barking" ringtone.

Endi answered, "Office of Herr Endicott. Who's calling please?" He used a heavy German accent and added, "Pay no attention to the dog. It is my guard dog."

"This is Joshua Tree with the Internal Revenue Service. Someone from this number called with a tip concerning tax fraud. I am trying to track down the caller."

Endi: "One moment please." He held the phone next to the car's radio speaker and turned the volume way up. It was playing salsa. He whispered to Padme and Coleman, "It's the IRS. I think we should tell them about Pinky's million-dollar bribe tomorrow."

Coleman: "Absolutely."

Endi turned the radio down, and still with the German accent said, "Mr. National Park, is it? Yes. Hum. Herr Endicott wants me to tell you that a city councilman named Pinky Blitz has been accepting bribes and is getting another one tomorrow during a press conference. Actually, a key to where the money is waiting for him. You might want to be at the Riviera on Isle of Venice Street off Las Olas around eleven tomorrow morning for a ribbon cutting and news conference. I would plan to follow him after the event." Endi disconnected.

20

Coleman, Endi, Padme, and Ohm caught the businessman's lunch special at the strip club called Gentlemen's Day Care. The doorman informed them that there was a two-drink minimum.

Coleman: "Can I have all six at the same time? I'm in training. My associates aren't drinking."

"Whatever. No dogs allowed except seeing eye. We don't get many seeing eye dogs in here. Not a popular spot for blind dudes." Har, har, har.

"Here's a hundred. The dog policy just changed. Come on, Ohm."

Padme to Coleman and Endi: "We need to look for someone wearing a cross. Or with a cross tattoo. Or cross earrings. Someone spiritual."

Coleman: "Who the hell cares if she is spiritual? I'd go for a Wicca transsexual if it was up to me."

Endi: "Or an Amazon warrior wearing a pointed brass bra and a spiked German helmet carrying a spear in one hand and a sword in the other."

Padme: "Because I will only work with spirit-seeking people."

Coleman: "Or the rich."

Padme: "Or the rich. What's our budget?"

Coleman: "Fifty thousand? Twenty-five apiece? I think we need two strippers." He looked at the squirmy gyrating sequined miniskirt on stage. He scooted a chair up closer. Looking over his shoulder at Padme, "I don't think we will have to stop at the dress store. What she is wearing is fine." The dancer winked at him and bent over grabbing her ankles, butt toward Coleman, and winked a sphincter.

The Rubenesque bleached-blond stripper with a large butt, breasts, and hips, but a miraculously narrow waist shuffled/wobbled over toward him on shoes with four-inch soles and eight-inch heels. Coleman worried that she was going to pitch over on to him.

"Oh, you have a little poodle. He's soooo cute!" Ohm growled at her. She let him smell her butt. He jumped on stage and vanished backstage where he caused some shrieking.

Coleman stuffed a Benjamin into her cleavage. Grinning, he looked at Padme and Endi behind him. The stripper squatted down to kiss him on the top of his head with her knees spread around his ears, her "possible" a foot from his face. He held out another hundred. She almost fell in his lap trying to let him put it wherever he wanted. After a few more winks, she sat on his lap, face-to-face, her knees around his waist and his face between her boobs. He whispered in her ear, "How'd you like to make twenty-five grand?"

"My name is Ready. Pleased to make your acquaintance. Should we head for a private room?" Her face was six inches from his. She licked his chin and brushed his lips with the tip of her tongue, and then she stuck her tongue in each ear lasciviously while pressing the back of his head between her breasts. She did a little shimmy and grinned at Padme and Endi over Coleman's shoulder. Coleman twisted around as far as he could. Padme could only see his eyes.

Padme thought she heard Coleman cry a muffled, "Haaaallllpppp!!!"

Ready ground her hips slowly to the music.

There was a new wave of barking and screaming backstage. Ohm ran out with a G-string in his mouth and ran around the brass pole playing keep-away from a tall blond trying to cover her bare boobs with one hand and possible with another. Gentlemen applauded thinking it was part of the act. Ohm sailed off the stage and hid in a dark corner stretching out for a good chew.

Ready sat on the stage with Coleman's face between her legs. Muffled by talcum-powdered thighs, eyes looking up at Ready's downturned face looking at him, Coleman mumbled, "Do you have a sister?"

"I have two sisters. Willing and Able. So you are that kind of boy?"

She let him breathe. He twisted around again and looked at Endi and Padme and asked them in a croak, "What about three girls?"

Padme said, "It's only money."

Ready asked, "Oh, one for each of you? Oh my, I haven't done a six-way in I don't remember how long."

Coleman looked up into her face. "It's not what you think."

Ready dropped her smile and seemed to age five years in a heartbeat. "Honey, that's what they all say."

Coleman: "Are you a single mother or a college student? Do you have a cross tattoo?"

Ready rolled her eyes: "Here we go. Ok, what do you want me to wear?"

Padme walked around Coleman carefully taking steps like she was on a runway in Paris modeling haute couture. She flashed an inch-thick wad of hundreds in Ready's face.

Ready let go of Coleman's head. "I am trying to get through college with two kids and an asshole husband who left me and I have an appointment this afternoon after the matinée to get a cross with Jesus crying blood-colored tears tattooed on my inner thigh. My major is veterinary medicine technology and I want to save all the animals in the world."

Padme: "Drugs?"

Ready: "You have this job, you take drugs."

Padme: "To the chase…all we want you to do is hand a certain politician an envelope with a key in it and say it's from Chicago. Tell him there is a phone number in the envelope to call for directions to where the key goes. If anyone asks, you know shit. I'm sure someone from the press will ask you. Just say some ugly dark greasy fat guy from Chicago gave you the envelope and some money to deliver the package."

Ready: "You want it to look like a bribe, huh? In front of the media?"

Padme looked over her shoulder at Coleman and Endi, and grinned. "This one will work."

Ready: "I went to beauty school but never finished, never been married, got no kids, and don't want no fucking tattoo of Jesus, but I do know how to make a politician squirm. And I ain't got no sisters. How much we talkin' again?"

Padme handed her the wad of hundreds. "Twenty-five thousand. This is maybe half. Count it later. You get the rest after completion of the mission."

Ready: "Lady, I would go down on a wildebeest and swallow for that kind of money, but I don't want no trouble with the mob."

Padme: "This guy is a city councilman and is evicting liveaboards to make way for condos owned by Northerners who don't even live here."

Ready: "Pinky Blitz?"

Padme: "Wow, nice guess."

Ready: "He's a regular. I've sat on his face a few times. I shouldn't have got up; should have choked him with a dirty brownie."

Padme: "He knows you? Even better."

"Well, he knows my pussy pretty well—I wouldn't bet on him knowing my face. My granny lived on a sailboat at one of those rent-a-slip liveaboard hotel-condos. Grandpa died. She was happy on that boat with her old dog. They took the dog away and put her in a home. Lady, I'd screw Pinky Blitz with a Roto-Rooter if you'll hold him down. When and where?"

Padme: "Tomorrow at eleven in the morning. The Riviera on Isle of Venice Street. Where shall we pick you up?"

Ready: "Say, you ever think about stripping? You want to audition right now? Follow me after my act and we'll find you an outfit."

Padme: "You know, I might like that. I have this idea with stilettos and a Sleep Number mattress, and a poodle."

Ready now on her knees with her boobs swinging like two pendulums in opposite directions: "Ok, new best friends, here's the deal. I wanna know what's really going on tomorrow. You're asking me to put my face on TV. The key? Does it have anything to do with drugs or a dead body? Come on. Not for any amount am I going to jail. They'd make me finish my GED in there for starters."

Padme to Coleman and Endi: "Either of you see any reason not to tell her?"

Endi: "A key to somewhere with a million bucks in it. That's all you need to know. You don't need to know where the somewhere is."

Ready: "What if he wants to marry me on the spot? Do I get half?"

Endi: "Do it quick. He's going to jail."

Ready: "I got to get my nails done. Buy some new underwear. Highlight my roots. Freshen my Brazilian. Pluck hair. Anal bleach tune-up. Touch up my areolar blush. Buy some shoes. Marrying money always has been Plan A. Plan B is see Plan A. Are you guys cops?"

Padme: "That a girl. Throw yourself into it. No, we're just concerned citizens acting strictly on our altruistic own."

The bouncer/doorman interrupted. "Ready, there are other customers. Not that these folks and their dog aren't just swell. But there are guys over there with hard-ons."

Ready: "Tiny, this is Coleman, Endi, and Padme. My new best friends. I won't be here for the lunch special tomorrow."

Coleman: "You may be seeing more of us. My partner and I are buying up these places all over the East Coast. Have you been in hospitality management long?"

Tiny: "And my grandfather is Warren Buffet."

21

"Holy crap, that's that gal I met." Zio drove into the Gentlemen's Day Care parking lot just as Padme got in the car. "My spiritual advisor! I'm following that car."

Popi: "You fucks said one dance, two drinks. At least."

Guido: "I'm gonna shoot you between the legs if you follow that car, Zio."

Zio: "Better go ahead, because that's what it is going to take to stop me."

Guido: "Now you know. She's just another white trash stripper."

Zio: "I can change her."

Popi: "What about my lap dance and cocktails? Besides, I got to take a dump." He rattled his chains for punctuation.

Endi was driving. Coleman had drunk all six of the drinks. Coleman was singing, "I…am…in…love…with…Ready…the…stripper!"

$ $ $

Endi: "There are three guys following us in a convertible."

Coleman: "Oh, stripper love. It is the purest kind of love.

I can imagine her being anything I want. Oh, the scent of powdered inner thighs. It's still in my nostrils. Warm perfume between those dirigibles. Soft, long, bleached-blond hair on my chest. Long black fingernails with glitter, unzipping my pants. Hot Doublemint breath and a moist tongue in my ear, fake eyelashes brushing my nipples…"

Padme: "God, Coleman, this is disgusting."

Endi said again: "We're being followed. Convertible with three guys. I'll stop. Someone get out and take their picture."

Coleman turned around, confirmed Endi's observation. Endi slammed on the brakes. Coleman hopped out. He had Padme's phone ready to snap a picture, but he had to wait until Popi managed to crawl back up onto the back seat of the convertible.

"Say cheese. You should keep those seat belts fastened." He ran back to the car.

Padme: "Gimme that phone. I think I recognize one of those guys." She looked at the picture of the three dazed men. "That big guy driving? I think I met him in a bar. He's probably just in love with me. I get this all the time—guys following me." They were on the move again.

Endi looking in the rearview mirror again: "The big guy is holding his nose. I guess he connected with the steering wheel. But he's keeping up. Well sort of. The guy in the back seat is standing up and thumping him on the head with a chain. Oops, there they go."

Coleman, his head turned around trying to see: "Where'd they go?"

Endi checking the mirror: "I don't know. They just aren't there anymore."

Padme: "These bar infatuations never last."

Coleman: "Speaking of, I could use a drink. My imagination is still dysfunctional. Need more alcohol on board. Once I start drinking it's all or nothing." He pulled out his breathalyzer. "Drinks in strip clubs are so watered down. I think we should make an offer on that titty bar. I really liked the layout. Remember, that was the first thing I said we should do with the money? And we should do Stripper-of-the-Month. Like Fruit-of-the-Month Club."

Endi: "We should not try to make any money. Every drink a double. Free peanuts. Dollar steaks. Free wings. Free rides home. It would be the first non-profit of its kind. Public service corporation. Call the girls therapists."

Coleman: "We can have exotic drinks like the Velvet Sausage Wallet."

Endi: "The Soggy Box."

"Snapper."

"Bat Cave."

"Lower Lips."

Padme: "STOP!" She covered Ohm's ears. "Don't listen to them, child."

Endi: "Weren't we going to open a strip club in the Bahamas on a mega yacht? With the Haitian brothers."

Coleman: "Why can't we do both?'

They high-fived each other. Endi slipped into a handicapped parking space at the front door of a liquor store.

22

Zio drove the convertible back to the Gentlemen's Day Care. He had lost the car he was following with Padme in it. Popi beating on him with chained wrists had caused him to drive off the road into a ten-foot ficus hedge. It had taken a while to get the car off the stubborn root system.

The bouncer at the door asked why the old guy was in chains.

Zio: "He's called the Kinkster. Tell the girls to watch out for him. He's fast. He touches inappropriately. That's why we have to keep him chained up."

"Two drink minimum."

Guido: "Of course."

Popi: "Rum and Diet Coke. No fruit. I gotta shit. Make them doubles. Where's the shitter?"

Zio to Guido: "You better go with him. He knows you better."

Guido: "How's he going to wipe his ass with his wrists chained in front of him?"

Zio: "Exactly."

Guido shouted: "TITTIES!" He was looking at the dancer on stage doing a headstand with her legs spread wide, her back against the brass pole. "I ain't wiping no Popi ass with a pair of milk cans like that to motorboat." The stripper dropped on her hands and knees and simulated being mounted by a stallion.

Zio handed Popi off to the doorman along with a hundred-dollar bill. "Another hundred if he doesn't run away. And another hundred if he comes back clean."

Zio and Guido took seats in front of the stage.

Zio said, "What's your name, Sugar Beet?" He held up a fifty to Ready on the stage above him.

"Ready for you, honey."

Zio: "That's nice. But what's your name? Never mind. You know who the two guys and the gal were that just left?"

Ready: "Gonna cost a lot more than fifty." The fifty disappeared somewhere, but for the life of him Zio couldn't figure out where it went…and she was practically naked.

Guido said, "The skinny blond gal that just left ten minutes ago? She is my spiritual advisor. I gotta find her."

Ready said out loud, "Here we go. Another fruitcake christer. Jesus."

A grinning Mexican two chairs down said, "I'm right here, amorcito. Jesus loves you."

Guido to Ready: "She's the most beautiful woman in the world."

Ready: "And I'm Kate Middleton, Duchess of Cambridge."

Zio to Ready: "Here's a hundred. Talk." To Guido: "This titty bar is getting expensive."

Ready: "You're gonna have to do better than that. I already got a stack of those from those three you're asking about."

Zio: "What do you mean a stack?"

Ready winked and proudly held her thumb and forefinger apart an inch. "Like that thick a stack." She was beaming. Her finest hour. Top of her game. Stripper Oscars. She pulled his head into her chest between her boobs and shimmied. The ecstasy was making her chatty and she didn't care.

Zio: "Then what you say I dance, and you tip me… you got all the money."

Ready moved over to Guido and got six inches from his face and asked demurely, "You have a girlfriend, big guy?"

"Nope." Guido threw a hundred on the stage. She squatted on it, and it disappeared.

Ready roughly grabbed Guido's crotch with one hand and kissed him with an open mouth, her heart precipitously pounding and her G-string suddenly wet. She sat on his lap, chest to chest, with her legs spread around his waist, and unbuttoned his shirt, then rubbed her nipples through his chest hair. She was suddenly short-of-breath horny. She whispered in his ear, "Are you getting hard, handsome?" She squirmed in his lap and licked his face. "To the private room." She extracted herself from his lap and led him by the hand toward the back of the club.

$ $ $

They gathered up Popi who was in a dark corner getting a lap dance. They had to pay his bill. Fourteen drinks and six lap dances. Another couple hundred for the cause.

Guido driving: "We follow her tomorrow. Her name is Ready. I think I'm in love. You're not going to believe this. She is supposed to give some bribe from my spiritual advisor and her two bodyguards to some crooked politician during a news conference tomorrow morning."

Popi: "You two are really starting to get on my nerves. How is this going to get my money back? I wasn't finished in there, goddamit."

Guido said, "Ready said the bribe was a million dollars."

Popi shouted: "That's my money. Turn the car around."

Guido to Zio: "I have no idea why we didn't leave him there, chained to a urinal."

Popi: "I'm ready to open a can of whoop-ass on you two. What does this have to do with my money?" He rattled his chains. "Boy, did that last one have a sweet pair of creamers on her!"

Zio turned around in his seat and stared directly in Popi's face and said: "You really don't get it. Who hires a stripper for twenty-five thousand to bribe a crook politician in public with a million dollars and why? And with whose money? It's not really a bribe. It is a lightning rod for a shit storm. They want him to take a fall for some reason. I don't give a shit about no stinking politician. I just can't help but think we are getting closer to that money. The million mysteriously given to the guy at that marina. Two assholes on a cruise ship with two million. And now supposedly a million to this politician. I think they have the twenty mil, and that they are using it to send messages. Making assholes lightning rods for the mob, or the IRS. I got the message. I'm thinking they found the boat and the money."

Guido: "Maybe we can follow the guy after the news conference, knock him on the head, and take the mil."

Zio: "If there actually is a million. We got to store Popi somewhere."

Popi: "I liked the titty bar. You can leave me there. Chain me to the stripper pole would be fine."

Guido: "We need Popi there tomorrow to see if he recognizes anyone."

Zio: "I can't believe that asshole took our picture with his phone."

Popi raking Zio's head with his wrist chains said: "I didn't get a good look at him as I had just been dumped on the floor of the car. Chupame la verga."

Guido backhanded the back seat blindly, missing Popi completely. Zio stood up on the front seat of the convertible and then stepped into the back seat. "Stop the fucking car. Pop the trunk." Guido pulled over and stopped. Zio grabbed the screaming Popi's ankle chain and dragged him out of the car. He threw Popi into the trunk and slammed the lid down.

$ $ $

At a red light, a vender came up to the convertible offering oranges and grapefruit. Popi was screaming and kicking the inside of the trunk lid.

Zio: "We're just taking the damn thing to the vet to be put down. It bit somebody. Were gonna have the head shipped to the lab for rabies."

23

The escaped Nixons stole a master pass card from housekeeping.

Jason (Surfer Nixon): "What time is it? This boat is a ghost ship." The sun was coming up.

Shawn (Druggie Nixon): Who cares? All kinds of rich comatose fuckers' livers are detoxing overdoses right now. We need some flash money."

Jason: "To the bridal suite for some clothes."

Shawn: "I want to find that CIA puke who took our wallets. And our millions."

Jason: "We'll ambush him. He won't be hard to find. He'll be looking for us."

Shawn: "Look for do not disturb signs. Those people probably just got to bed. Their purses, and pants with wallets in them, are probably on the floor where they dropped them trying to get in bed before they passed out on the floor. They will be dead to the world. If they wake up, just say maid service…sorry, and run."

The Nixons robbed eighteen rooms in less than thirty minutes. No occupants so much as rolled over. They rallied in the bridal suite. Dressed in designer jeans, their fancy shoes, polo shirts, and sweaters tied around their necks like scarves, sunglasses, and boat captain hats, they headed for the outdoor breakfast buffet poolside. The servers were setting up the buffet.

They each had a pillowcase full of booty they had stolen. They sat at an isolated table next to the rail.

"Coffee and mimosas for the two of us, please," Shawn politely asked the waiter. "Make the mimosas doubles."

Jason: "And we'll do the buffet. Could we please have some water too?" An aside to Shawn, "That cooking sherry leaves a mean aftertaste. I am epic dehydrated."

As they slugged mimosas and wolfed food, they emptied wallets and threw them overboard. There were two passports in their haul.

Jason: "Hey, did you notice that there is a helicopter down there on the ass end of this boat?"

Shawn: "And you're thinking what I'm thinking? Why the hell is it pink?"

Jason: "What I'm thinking is realize our multitudinous money, corrupt the pilot, and disappear nippily."

Shawn: "After mealtime and a second pot of coffee of course."

Jason: "Unequivocally."

Shawn: "What's your take so far? I got only a couple of thou in cash. Do we keep a credit card or three?"

Jason: "I got a big bag of poker chips. The guy must have done pretty well at the casino last night. Plus, some gold chains. And probably ten grand in cash. Not bad for a half hour's work."

Shawn: "You think we can cash in the chips when the casino opens and get away with it?"

Jason: "That's plan A." The waiter delivered more drinks. "When does the casino open?"

"It's always open, sir."

$ $ $

They headed to the purser's desk. A sleepy assistant that didn't know them was on duty. They reported the theft of their identification and money and asked if it was true that there was a CIA agent on board. And could they possibly arrange to consult with said agent as their missing gold, diamonds, and cash, that they were couriering to one of the stops on the ship's itinerary (the gold belonged to the direct heir of Pablo Picasso), was part of a considerable donation to the Sisters of Weeping Orphanage, to the reverend mother Abbess, who was the sister of New York's mayor, and owned one-quarter of the land that the Empire State Building stood on? And could we have another room as we are afraid to go back to our room?

They each gave the purser a one-hundred-dollar bill.

The purser thought, *you can't make that shit up at seven in the morning.* "Of course. May I have your passports?"

Jason: "Don't be cheeky. Don't you get it? We were fucking robbed in our sleep. They took the passports too." He looked at Shawn: "You think we should do a ship-to-shore and call Charlie 'Mad Dog' Garotta and inform him of our loss? See what he can do to motivate this mark?"

Shawn: "I'd say call Leoni 'Cutcherheadoff' Flossie. He does the out-of-town persuasion work."

Jason: "Where is our next port of call? Can you put in a call to Chicago for us? We lost our cell phones too, and iPads."

Jason to Shawn: "Our organization *has* sued a cruise line before, haven't we?"

Purser: "I don't need passports. I hope this room will be adequate." He handed a key card to each Nixon. "I do need your names."

Jason: "No you don't."

"No, I don't."

"Ok, the name's Nixon. I'm Richard, and this is Thelma Patricia."

"You can call me Pat."

Jason handed the purser another hundred. "We're probably getting off at the next stop. You won't have to worry your pretty little head about this for very long. Capiche?"

Jason: "Come on. I need a shower."

Shawn: "Just ask the CIA agent to come to the new room, will ya?"

Purser: "When would be convenient for you?"

Jason: "Give us time to freshen up. Say nine thirty?"

Purser: "Excellent, sirs."

Shawn: "Give that man another Benjamin, pard."

As Jason handed over another one-hundred-dollar bill, he asked, "And can we have the room number of the pilot of that pink helicopter on the ass end of the boat?"

"That'll be another hundred."

"That'll be pushing your luck exponentially."

"I agree, Mr. Nixon. Give me a moment." He wrote a room number on a sticky note and handed it to Jason.

Purser: "I don't suppose having the IRS agent join you two would be useful as well?" The purser knew how to fish for souls.

Jason and Shawn: "IRS agent?!"

Purser: "He is part of the team."

Jason and Shawn: "Team?!"

Purser: "FBI and the IRS often work as a team. I'm thinking another five hundred."

Jason: "I'm agreeing. I don't suppose this IRS agent has anything to do with a rather large amount of cash."

Purser with his palm out: "So I heard. I saw him dancing and entertaining five of our widows who are traveling together last night. I would imagine he is currently asleep, surely being exhausted as he and the ladies shut down the place, I heard. You might find him in..." He discretely wrote a room number on a sticky note.

Jason counted out five more Benjamins.

Jason to Shawn on the way to their new accountant: "We should probably cut back on drug usage in the future some. It's kind of interesting being able to think."

24

When Ready answered her cell phone, she sounded like Beelzebub, one of the seven princes of hell. Padme was outside the trailer ready to pick her up. Ready showed how an exotic, physically fit, binge-trained twenty-three-year-old can rally.

"All I got to do is brush my tusks and pee. I'm there. Watch out, Pinky. This time you better wear a snorkel."

She took two hits of marijuana, two Adderalls, two tramadols, and grabbed a two-liter of Mountain Dew. "I'll dress on the way."

$ $ $

Padme convinced Endi and Coleman that there was no need for the three of them to expose themselves at a televised press conference. Either Ready would make it happen or not. It really didn't matter. They would find out on the news in due time. If she didn't make it happen, they would plan a new prank. That was the fun part anyway.

They weren't there for the show.

Ready was not as stable on the platform stilettos as she should have been, thanks to her fragile blood chemistry. Her turquoise ocean scene miniskirt was so tight that she could only take six-inch steps. It was ten yards to the microphones. In her hurry, ankles threatened to buckle. Men rushed to her aid. She slowed down. She wore a two-foot diameter straw hat with a ribbon halfway down her back and dark glasses with lenses three inches wide. A frivolous breeze off the canal caused the ribbon to wave in her eyes every fourth or fifth step.

It was all too much even for an athlete, and Ready went down. A kind gentleman made a grab, snagging the highway-orange tank top. A D flopped. As she fell backwards into another man's arms, the skirt rode up exposing a string thong leaving little to the imagination. She jettisoned the sun hat and straightened her sunglasses. She put everything back where it belonged.

Even in blindingly sunny Florida, photographers seemed to need strobes. A young wannabe photojournalist, holding a strobe, got knocked into the pool. Witness said they saw St. Elmo's fire between her teeth before the electrical system shorted out, taking out the microphone on the podium with it.

Ready finally kicked off her heels and barefooted it to Councilman Pinky Blitz and handed him the envelope. Cameras flashed as she kissed him hard and long while trying to unzip his pants.

Watching from the sidelines, Boner Bonadonna read the handwriting on the wall and disappeared.

$ $ $

Joshua Tree of the IRS stood dumfounded in the midst of protesters, the press, and onlookers. He was only ten feet from the struggling Pinky. Ready's nose cones were acting like a pair of rowdy St. Barnard puppies. Pinky threw his arms up in the air as he tried backing up. Agent Tree pulled out his badge and grabbed the envelope from Pinky. "I'll take that."

Pinky didn't notice. He was trying to get Ready off of him. Ready slipped to her knees furiously working on his zipper. Joshua Tree backed into the crowd. Ready straddled Pinky's face and sat down hard and squeezed. Pinky's legs and feet kicked in a blur as police officers tried to pull her off, her head buried in his crotch. They didn't realize that they were dealing with a professional exotic dancer with thighs as tuned as a professional wrestler, and a vagina that could pick up a longneck bottle of beer, take the cap off, and suck it dry. As they tried to drag her off, Pinky's face came too. There was muffled screaming for a few more seconds and then the noise and kicking stopped. Ready sat a little harder.

They finally pulled her off Pinky. He was blue.

"Someone call 911."

The show was over. Joshua Tree blended into a palm tree and vanished with the envelope. He climbed into his black Crown Vic and turned up the AC. He was drenched with sweat. He wiped his face and as the air turned cool, he opened the envelope. There was a key in it with a tag tied to it and a phone number written on it. There was a poem:

Dear Pinky,
A million to you
Keep up the good work
Which you got to do
Or forget the perk
And find your feet in concrete goo.
Just call the number,
Follow the directions to wealth.
A paycheck to remember…
Do as you're told or lose your health,
Breathing seawater, no air to render.

"That is the worst poem I have ever read in my life."

Guido saw the black guy in a suit, with Ready's envelope in his hand, get into a black Crown Vic with government plates on it.

They pulled up behind the Crown Vic. Guido got out. He stepped up to the driver's side window. He lightly tapped on the window, which slid down a few inches. "Help you?"

Guido: "What happened there?"

The window came down the rest of the way. Joshua Tree said, "I don't really know. Some crazy bitch tackled the guy that was getting some kind of recognition or announcing another condo project and they went down and she wouldn't get off of him. There were a bunch of demonstrators. I think he's a city councilman. Hey, it's Florida. Who knows?"

Guido saw the poem and the key with the tag on it on the driver's lap. He blindsided Joshua Tree with a punch to the temple, reached in over the slumping figure, grabbing the key, the note, and the envelope.

He got back in the convertible on the passenger side and said to Zio, who was behind the wheel, "We best vaporize."

Zio: "Outta here." He shot the convertible into traffic amid multiple horns.

Popi: "I smell money. Where is it? Gimme the letter. Turn around."

Guido called the number.

25

The Nixons found James Bond spread-eagled on his bed with his ankles and wrists tied with neckties to the bed. He was wearing panties and a bra. He had a nylon stocking over his head. His nose was smashed by the tight stocking. He was breathing through his mouth; he was breathing steadily. Shawn poked him but he didn't respond other than licking his lips and farting.

Jason: "Here's my wallet. Looks like he burned through a lot of my $50K."

Shawn: "A badge; that may come in handy." He was opening drawers.

Jason: "Before we leave, we should order room service for him. Maybe a continental breakfast and a pot of coffee?"

Shawn: "He's gonna need it. And here is a gun. Well, well."

"And a cell phone!"

Jason put a door hanger on the chest of the passed-out agent. It said, *Maid: Please Service.*

Shawn: "Let's lose his pants and shoes. Just another complication."

Jason opening the glass sliding door to the little deck said, "Just toss them overboard." They looked in the closet and found the black fatigues and combat boots and threw them over the side too.

$ $ $

They found Peabody sandwiched between two widows in corsets, high heels, and stockings. There were clothes spread everywhere. A bottle of baby oil had spilled on the bedside table. A lamp was knocked over. A wig was hanging on the other lamp. The sliding door to the private deck was open and Shawn saw another completely naked widow throwing up over the railing.

Jason: "It's Shrek naked. Enucleate me."

Shawn poked at the sleeping widows. They stirred. One eye opened, then the other. "Oh shit, Thelma." She elbowed the other viciously.

Shawn: "Get dressed, ladies. Holy crap, Peabody, these two are old enough to be your mother."

First widow: "Shut that cock-pocket Twinky. You want a turn in the barrel?"

Second widow: "Thelma Jean!"

First widow: "You haven't had a knob-gobble till you've had one with dentures removed. Ready to play slurp-the-gherkin, little man?"

They finally herded all three widows into the hall and threw their stuff out with them.

Jason: "Holy crap, that was ambitious. Like wouldn't it be cool to have a granny like that!"

Peabody: "I gotta shit. Right now." He disappeared in a heartbeat, and rematerialized on the toilet. There was a staccato burst of gas propelled turdettes splashing, then liquid splashing, then a ten-second fart that sounded like an idling inboard exhaust under water.

Shawn: "Epic bust-ass, Peabody!"

They heard two dry heaves…then the exhaust fan turned on. Flushing. A weak, "Oh, God."

Jason: "Don't come out until you take a shower. You surely soiled yourself. You got two minutes."

They heard the shower running. Two minutes. They looked in. Peabody was passed out in the tub with the shower on his face. Jason turned it total cold.

Shawn: "That Pea can really move." Peabody had bolted out of the tub and sat back down on the toilet.

Peabody: "What do you want?" He squinted his eyes and strained, grunting. Nothing happened.

Jason: "We better check for a prolapse. He might need a doctor. You feel anything hanging in the water that shouldn't be Pea?"

Shawn: "Ok, had your fun. Open your eyes and look at me. What do you see?" He conked Peabody on the top of the head with the barrel of the gun.

Peabody: "A Glock 9?"

Shawn: "Wow, that's good."

Jason: "Skills! Well then, maybe you know what we want."

Peabody: "Give me a few. Gotta make sure the purge is done. Then I'll take you to your money." He farted. More grease. "I think I better do the shower one more time."

Fifteen minutes later, a frail, but dressed, Peabody was leading the Nixons to the safe in the ship's business office.

$ $ $

Jason: "What we do with the Pea?" The three were standing on the promenade deck by the rail.

Shawn: "Overboard?"

Peabody: "I gotta come with you. I'm your hostage now. Besides, I can launder our money. You'll get caught again. I got skills. You need me."

Jason: "Our money?"

Shawn: "He has a point. We could use an accountant. We haven't exactly managed our money too well up to this point, you got to admit."

Peabody: "Twenty-five percent. I go my way, you go yours. Your way will be Central America and a life of entitlement. My life will be back to work like nothing happened. I escaped with my life—I'm a hero—sort of. But I'll have nice vacations annually in Grand Cayman."

Shawn: "We'll think about it."

Peabody: "We gotta do something about that federal agent. The guy is a real chode."

Shawn: "I think choder-boy is not problematic at this point in time, considering the historical drama in his stateroom."

Jason: "Tell you what, Pea…we're gonna give you fifty thousand. Just enough for some fun, but not enough to be a red flag. We're gonna put you in that lifeboat up there, gagged and tied up. Or rather you are going to go up there and gag and tie yourself up. When you hear the pink helicopter lift off you can miraculously get yourself free and tell them Somali pirates overpowered you, conked you on the head, shot you, took all the money, got back on their boat, tied you up, you're lucky to be alive, all that…" Jason counted out fifty thousand then threw in an additional wad of fifties, twenties, and tens. Still holding it, he said, "I believe that is more than generous."

Shawn: "Yes, above all, we want to be remembered as generous. We'll even conk you on the head again to add authenticity."

Peabody: "What about James Bond? And what you mean the Somalis shot me?"

"Come here." He grabbed Pea and bent him over the rail. "I'm gonna shoot you in the ass." Jason grabbed a cushion from a deck chair and wrapped it around the gun to silence it. Shawn put another cushion over Peabody's face as Jason fired a bullet grazing Pea's ass. The nine-millimeter projectile disappeared into the ocean. The muzzle blast caused more damage than the bullet. He threw the gun in the ocean. Pea passed out on the deck.

They propped him up in a deck chair between them. They didn't have to wait long. Peabody woke up winding up for a marathon scream. Shawn stuffed the corner of a towel in his mouth. He soiled himself again.

Eyes wide open. Clawing and attempting to escape. A little more soiling.

Shawn said, "Now Pea, before you bleed and shit all over the place, climb up there and hide in that lifeboat. There will be a first aid kit on board, I bet. And food. You can have a leisurely breakfast. You know what to do. Don't forget your $50K." He stuffed the money in Peabody's pockets. "You promise not to scream if I let you talk?" To Jason: "I think he shat himself epically again."

Peabody: Vigorous head nodding. They pulled the gag.

Peabody: "Son of a bitch my ass is killing me you fucks. I can't believe you did that. I never been shot before. I'm an accountant. We don't get shot."

Shawn: "You do if you're working with the mob."

Peabody: "I don't work for the mob."

In unison: "You do now."

Jason: "Start climbing. Put some Neosporin on that nasty wound. Wouldn't want your ass to abscess off."

Shawn: "Yea, that would be a real pain in the ass." Har, har, har.

26

Coleman, Endi, and Padme watched the coverage of the press conference on the news. There was no mention of the bribe. The talking head reported that Mr. Pinky Blitz had to be intubated and put on a respirator on the way to the hospital. He also suffered a broken nose and has been admitted for overnight observation. Mr. Blitz was not available for comment.

Ready was shown being taken away by two cops. She had handcuffs on.

A clever reporter found out the assailant, a Ready Sloan, worked at the Gentlemen's Day Care, and the reporter interviewed one of Ready's co-workers who said Pinky liked to have his face sat on. And that he was considered a better-than-average tipper. And that he and Miss Sloan sort of had an ongoing relationship. Sugar daddy; sugar baby.

Coleman: "Well, that was certainly unsatisfying. And I went to all that trouble writing that poem too."

Endi: "Maybe somebody found the letter and key. I hope a reporter found it."

Endi's phone rang.

Zio: "Whoever this is that was the worst poem I have ever read in my life."

Endi: "Way to break the ice, there. Don't be so hurtful until you get to know me. Poetry is my only therapy."

Zio: "Yea? You need a new therapist. Ok, what the fuck is going on? Was this letter supposed to be some kind of bribe in public for that dickhead council member? Delivered by the trash-stripper-bimbo to add insult to injury?"

Endi: "All your lights are on at the top floor. And how did you come into the possession of my poetry?"

Zio: "Ok, my new spiritual advisor, she says, put nice out, you get nice back. Sorry about the crack about your poetry. It was swell. I picked the letter up off the ground."

Endi: "Sounds like my spiritual advisor too. What you put out there you get back."

Zio: "What goes around comes around."

Endi: "Hey, maybe we got the same one."

Zio: "Ok pal, mi casa, su casa, and all that. The first line of your POS poem mentions a million. And I'm assuming it was for Pinky Blitz. He's in the business. I'm in the business. I assume you are in the business. We think you got some of our money. We're missing twenty gigantic, and Chicago and South America are breathing down our necks. Now, one businessman to another, let's parlay here, what you say?"

Endi: "I have no idea what you are talking about, friend."

Zio: "How about a couple of million found in a mattress by a pair of long-haired hippie freaks that joined a Carnival cruise a couple of days ago? How about a guy named Macro Salsa and a million in a duffel bag and partying until he dropped at Lightningbolt Marina and Lounge? How about a guy named Boner Bonadonna who owns Lightningbolt Marina and Lounge at the news conference? And a stripper I met at the *Gentlemen's Day Care* being paid $25K to sit on Pinky's face and deliver a bribe for the five o'clock news? How about me taking a wild guess that you found a Sea Ray with my Chicago family's belongings in it? How about some dude in a big black Crown Vic with government plates snatching the letter out of Pinky's hand? How about me taking it from the dude in the Crown Vic?"

Endi hung up. He looked at Padme and Coleman. "Oh, crap. I think I know who was following us. I think I got their picture even."

Padme: "The guy from the bar that followed me? Us?!"

Endi: "Yea, he ended up with the envelope. I think he's connected. A soldier for Chicago no less."

Coleman: "Time to flee to a desert island I know."

Endi: "He knows about the Sea Ray."

The phone rang again.

Endi answered: "You driving a convertible with an old guy in the back seat in chains?"

Zio: "We do have the same spiritual advisor. I didn't know she worked as a stripper. Never seen her there before at the Day Care. Funny, she don't look the type. She must be new."

Endi: "She's not."

Zio: "Maybe we could do a three-way sometime soon."

Endi: "Trust me, I'm not that kind of girl."

Zio: "I mean on the phone, numb nuts. Or a meet. Let her keep us from accidently killing each other. We got mutual interests. I hit a button when I brought up that Sea Ray, huh?"

Silence.

Zio: "See?"

Endi: "I'll talk to my associates and call you back. This number, ok?"

Zio: "Yea. You better. I'm gonna go bail Ready Sloan out of jail and ask her a few polite questions. I think she knows you. I'm gonna instruct her to wait to involve you with this whole sordid affair on a hunch we might have mutual interests. You should be bailing her out. Not me. She works for you. She's looking at an assault charge. You put her up to it. You're going to jail too."

Endi: "Risking her wrath, Ready didn't actually accomplish the mission."

Zio: "I'm quite sure even the least dangerous detective on the planet would perk up if he hears who sent Ready on the mission in the first place."

Endi: "I am thankful, sir."

Zio: "I'll take care of Ready. See, how's that for what you put out there you get back? You're supposed to trust me now a little. What's my spiritual advisor's name?"

"Padme."

Zio: "Tell her I'm trying to change for the better. I'm serious. This work is thwarting my grasp for serenity. I need another session with her."

They both hung up.

Endi: "Padme, you should start a church and offer hospice care for Special Olympic greasers. We could launder some money for you."

Coleman: "I still say we need to flee to the islands…
right now."

Padme: "I never met you assholes. I'm outta here.
Mount up, Ohm."

$ $ $

Coleman fired up the twin Chevys in the Chris-Craft
and the old boat made its first all-out run, cigarette-boat
style, to the Bahamas (best she could do at 4500 RPMs
was fifteen knots). They burned ninety-five gallons of
gas, but they got home by cocktail hour. Their visit to
Fort Lauderdale had been a non-event as there was no
immigration record of them being there.[10]

$ $ $

The next morning there was an explosion heard on
the ocean side of the island. As long as there is just one
explosion, and none following it, the islanders do not place
any significance on it. And really, it wasn't that loud. It
was more of a: phuurummfffh.

Coleman and his dad in the late 70s had found a missile

---

10 Coleman has been going back and forth between Conch Key and Florida
by boat his whole life without passing through either U.S. or Bahamian
immigration. One time when he was a kid he got caught in a strong westerly
breeze on a Hobie Cat sailboat and couldn't tack it back to Conch Key so
just sailed on to Florida. He called his dad, who came over on the cruiser
(reluctantly) and picked him up, and they dragged the little catamaran sailboat
back to Conch Key behind them. Dad wasn't happy, but had to admit that
he had not noticed that young Coleman wasn't around and was glad he had
survived his night at sea.

that had been launched from Cape Canaveral whose propellant hadn't been kept dry. It fizzled. His dad had been tracking all launches from Canaveral through the sixties and seventies hoping and planning for that very day. The other three SAMs (surface-to-air missiles) that were fired at the same time destroyed their targets a hundred miles out to sea. This one splashed in twenty feet of water halfway between Conch Key and Marsh Harbor.

He and his dad had the warhead off and buried in just three hours. It went in a pre-dug hole in the jungle on vacant land that his dad had bought next to the house. (You just never know when you might need to bury something in a hurry. Dad always kept a deep hole handy.) The warhead weighed a hundred pounds. His dad identified it as an M248 composition B-HE blast/fragmentation. It was designed to be exploded high in the sky next to an enemy aircraft inbound to the USA, using a proximity fuse, and was designed to obliterate airplanes with basically a load of flak. Dad taught son how to disarm the proximity fuse. They saved the fuse (never know).

Officials back then found the missile sans warhead. Raytheon blamed Hughes, and RCA blamed Raytheon, and Hughes blamed the Air Force, and the Air Force blamed NASA. The final conclusion was that the warhead had fallen off the missile somewhere during its troubled trajectory, and that it was at least a mile deep in the Atlantic.

The next morning, after Coleman and Endi had returned from Florida, the old warhead blew the sunken Sea Ray, the *Master Baiter,* into thousands of pieces. It basically became sand. Dust to dust. The density of the water surrounding the blast actually prevented the explosion from doing much damage to reefs or underwater wildlife; the debris and shrapnel fragments' energy momentum came to a complete stop in less than a thirty-foot radius. Of course, a geyser of water seventy feet high was observed by Endi and Coleman when Coleman pushed the button as they were sitting on the sand with binoculars and Bloody Marys.

No one on the island apparently saw the blast except them because no one ever mentioned it. Or, since no one wants to be a lightning rod on Conch Key, even if they did see it, they just didn't want to get involved—none of their business. And there is no media on the island to ask questions, report, blame, scare, and make up end-of-the-world scenarios. And the last thing anybody on Conch Key wanted was to have officials swarming the island like in the seventies when Cape Canaveral lost that missile.

27

Jason: "Why is the helicopter pink? You are the only person so far that we have run into on this entire floating roulette wheel that doesn't seem to be a carnal deviant. Is your name really Taco?"

"It's really Tabitha. When I was dancing, my stage name was Taco. Dow Corning used my tatas as templates for breast replacements. Breast cancer is a huge part of my life. I get these rebuilt every couple of years in Costa Rica. Wanna see them?" She cupped her breasts with her hands and jiggled them.

Shawn: "Sure!"

Jason: "Sure!"

Taco unbuttoned her blouse.

Shawn: "Lumpatious!"

Jason: "Blastoising!"

Shawn to Jason: "Jason, you ought to get a pair of those."

Jason: "Taco, you ever think about getting another pair on your back?" To Shawn: "Would that be the perfect woman or what?"

Taco: "I'll do it the same day you get a penis on your chin."

Har, har, har.

Taco: "I'm a 501c3. I don't like to pay taxes. I even changed my name to Udder."

Jason: "You especially wouldn't be happy about paying taxes if you saw your IRS agent and his herd of old ladies this morning. What does Udder mean?"

Taco: "Mount up. Let me see if I can get this POS running. Throw the money in the back. There are bungees. Don't want it blowing out; bungee it down." She started pumping things and flipping switches using all of her hands and feet at the same time. She was barefoot. "When I get this thing running you won't be able to hear a thing. Any last words?" That was the extent of her passenger pre-flight briefing. The boys were frantically trying to figure out the seat belts.

Shawn: "Yea. Airsick bags?"

Taco: "Don't need them. You puke, I do an evasive maneuver. It's a steep bank with a severe slip away from the flying vomit. Haven't got any on me all these years of flying. You don't want to vomit if you can help it." She put on a headset. None for the passengers.

Taco waited for the stern of the *Ecstasy* to peak in its rise cycle then she pulled, pushed, kicked, twisted, hands, legs, feet. The helicopter didn't hover, climb, or turn. It just blasted off straight toward Key West at 100 knots.

Knockers Helicopter Charter left deck chairs, towels, glassware, umbrellas, cushions, plates, sunglasses, hats, robes, flip-flops, suntan lotion, beach bags…all flying in vortexes or careening into the ocean.

28

Pinky was back at his estate sipping a rum and pineapple juice through a straw. He was wearing a neck brace. He had a plaster on his nose. Both eyes were black and blue and half swollen shut. Bonadonna was across from him. They were in Pinky's private office on the second floor.

Boner: "Shit, you're lucky to be alive. You gonna probably have clap in your nose."

Pinky: "They got me on Zithromax. This ain't my first rodeo."

Boner: "Wonder what was in the envelope?"

Pinky: "The cops said Ready told them that some greaser from Chicago gave it to her and that she was told it had a key in it and a note with a phone number—that's all she knew. And the hood gave her some money to do the deed on me. The key supposedly went to a storage locker that supposedly had a million in it. I was supposed to call the number to get the storage locker's location." He started coughing until he began sloshing his drink on himself. Boner took the glass just in time. Boner pounded the doubled over Pinky on the back.

Pinky's face turned bright red and his oxygen cannula

fell out. He exhaled curse words with each panting breath. Boner tried to put the cannula back; Pinky swatted his hand away.

Pinky: "I can't stop smelling that pussy. Last thing I remembered before everything went black was that thing squeezing my nose shut. I already couldn't open my mouth. I thought I was going to actually die. I damn near did." Cough. "This whole thing is bullshit. There never was any money. Like making it look like I was taking bribes. Jeeze. I'm just helping the city take out the trash. These liveaboard boat people are just trashy garbage. Half the boats they live on are derelicts. The pieces of shit boats haven't left their slips for years. I'm just doing urban renewal." He coughed again, gasped, and croaked, "Shit, reminds me when the priest had to do the Heimlich on me during communion. Don't let one of them wafers go down wrong." He wiped the tears from his eyes and sipped his drink. "Had to grab the chalice of wine. Drank the whole thing. Would a thought I crucified Jesus myself they were so pissed off."

Boner: "I hear ya brother. I'd be happy to sell Lightningbolt Marina for condos. Just waiting for an offer. The liveaboards at my place are worse than trailer park trash. And I got to deal with them every day of my life. They all think they are *Miami Vice* living on a boat, and want to keep an alligator, and a Glock. Unbelievable. And we need to keep the concrete business legit—keep those condos coming."

Pinky took a sip and held the glass up: "Here's to the concrete business and condos—keep Florida strong. No one knows where the envelope went. Cops are looking for it. I think Ready was also using the press conference to showcase her acting ability. Get her twat on TV. Like I said, I don't think there was nothing in the envelope."

Boner: "She got out of jail the same day. We sent a guy over to talk to her at the strip club, but her bodyguard said we had to make an appointment and pass a security clearance first. Her performances are sold out for two weeks."

Pinky: "My point exactly. She heard about Macro Salsa at your shop getting a million and made this whole thing up. Classic publicity stunt. That's what I think. Stupid Macro probably stuffed her full of Benjamins himself and helped her hatch the plan."

Boner: "So I went over there personally today for the matinee. See what I could do to talk to the bitch—you know, help you out. This kind of shit needs to stop. I don't think that thing with Macro Salsa was just a publicity stunt. Someone was out to make us lightning rods for drug mob lightning. And they are spending money to do it. Her brand-new bodyguard, who it turns out I actually know from my juvi years, said Ready has a lot of flash money. Somebody, two men and a woman, gave her a huge stack of hundreds to deliver the envelope. She's been taking in tips of over five grand a night with her newfound public admirers, he says. And who knows what her percentage off the gate is? And that's not counting the autographed photos, T-shirts, used G-strings, and all that. She's got sponsors for chrissake—like massage parlors and escort services and limos and crotch-less underwear and vibrators. I could keep going. I wouldn't be surprised if Johnson & Johnson trys for an endorsement for KY. I guess she bought a bathtub-sized, stemmed, clear, plastic champagne glass and takes a bubble bath in it on stage. You can buy a private showing of her taking a shower afterward. We probably ought to take in the show as soon as you're recovered."

"What's Chicago sayin'?" Pinky asked.

"Funny you should ask. I haven't heard a word."

The desk phone rang. "Boss, there are two Oriental dudes down here saying they got an appointment. You want, I should send them up?" Pinky heard a single gunshot. He dove under the desk.

EPILOGUE

So…how did all this end?

Zio got an e-mail with a photo of Boner and Pinky (Pinky still in his neck brace) glowering at the camera. They were standing in five-gallon paint buckets, arms apparently tied behind their backs. Two Orientals in ball caps and oversized sunglasses stood on each side of them. The Orientals were smiling and waving at the camera.

$ $ $

Joshua Tree could not generate any interest with his supervisors for the envelope, poem, and key. Even he didn't care. The envelope, poem, and key were hermetically sealed in shrink-wrap and sent for storage in a no-longer-mined section of a salt mine 650 feet under Hutchinson, Kansas, where George Clooney's Batman's costume is kept in perpetuity.

Padme convinced Coleman and Endi that using the treasure for revenge would only cause someone to seek revenge on them. "What you put out there you get back" (Law One of the Cosmos, according to Padme). She took them in an opposite direction, one of life-heightening and quietude; they started the much-needed, non-profit, online newsletter *Rum Recalls,* which follows their non-profit organization Rum-Buy-Gum, which regulates the impurities allowed, and minimum alcohol content, in local rums made on the small islands of the East Indies.

Padme got ordained online by the Universal Church of California (UCC). It took five minutes. The UCC is the most ecumenical of all the online churches in its theology; perfect for Padme as she, to this day, continues to work through the cornucopia of spiritual possibilities that the universe has to offer. UCC's credo is *God must love diversity; look at all the religions out there.* They offer a huge online selection of pastoral paraphernalia, including items blessed by such spiritual leaders such as the Dalai Lama's cousin; Pope Benedict XVI's daughter; Bishop Tutu's retired compere; C.S. Lewis' great-granddaughter's coven leader; and Mary Baker Eddy's physician's anthropologist daughter.

The crew bought a bank in Tightwad, Missouri, called the Tightwad Bank and Trust. The Ozarks. The town has a population of sixty-nine people, thirty-one households, and eighteen families. Tightwad is located very close to Truman Lake, a huge reservoir whose water level fluctuations can differ as much as thirty feet depending on the year. The water is used to keep the adjoining lake, Lake of the Ozarks, level. Peabody and his bride, the widow "Wife of Shrek," also an accountant, run the bank and control the water flow from lake to lake. (They receive a large annual remuneration from the Association of Marina Owners of the Lake of the Ozarks.) When interviewed by the *Washington Post* about the Tightwad Bank and Trust,

Mrs. Peabody said, "We're seeking customers with a sense of humor."

Because of its name, the Tightwad Bank has depositors from all over the world just to have checks with that name on it. Because of its location, it is basically below the radar of every bank examiner who ever has had the misfortune to have it under their scrutiny (no one can find it, much less take it seriously). Money laundering there is state of the art. The bank services accounts from all fifty states and 196 countries. Deposits are over 600 million.[11]

$ $ $

Guido and Popi own a fleet of drones they operate from multiple gyro-stabilized houseboats between Cuba and the Florida Keys that use their roofs as a landing strip. Working closely with defrocked employees of Garmin, and bankrolled by the Tightwad Bank and Trust, the vessels remain stationary in international waters using the ECDIS navigation system that controls thrusters strategically located all around the

---

11 That is not including the various non-profit religious trusts that maintain balances that are not accountable to any country's IRS scrutiny. These include examples such as: the Catholic Prostate-Care Sponsor Foundation; the Episcopal Global Animal Balanoposthitis Relief Fund; the Baptist Far-East-India-Calf-Enteritis Project; the Baptist Great Lakes Rust Removal Action Research Effort; The Canadian Pentecostal Million Man Ice Fishing For Jesus League; the Methodist More-Methodists-By-Donor-Base-Understanding-Precedent; NMBLA (National Man Boy Love Association); the Conch Island Temperance Woman's Club; the Conch Island Men's Repeal Prohibition Effort; the South East Florida Full Nudity Freedom Of Expression Council PAC; the Strippers' Thong-of-the-Month Club; and the Randers Denmarcian Cleansing Enema Center…to name a few.

hull. They are always pointed into the wind. The drones that are launched and recovered from their decks legitimately offer services such as search and rescue air coverage, weather real time, tsunami and hurricane early warnings, currents and temperatures, and smuggling operation surveillance. They are subject to occasional navigation failures and end up in Cuba. The little black planes have a droppable pod with a payload of one hundred pounds, or approximately 4.5 million in U.S. hundred-dollar bills.

Popi regained favor with Chicago with this drone service. Chicago teamed with their Japanese counterpart (the Yakuza) to provide similar operations between Japan and South Korea, as well as Taiwan and mainland China. Chicago also teamed with the "mother" family in Sicily for similar operations all over the Mediterranean mostly transferring currency. (The family meets operating expenses just playing the currency exchange market!)

Popi never returned to his wife. She was sent a million dollars and a death certificate for Popi so she could get on with her life. Padme insisted. Put out there what you want back.

$ $ $

Padme and Guido were married in India at the Taj Mahal by Gandhi's second wife's nephew who had been saved by Jesus (Himself in Person), he claimed. They got married four times; at six a.m., noon, six p.m., and midnight. Thus, there were four receptions. They came in on a painted sacred cow, which attended all four services, with her calf by her side (also painted nicely, but he was not housebroken so ended up being banished for the midnight service especially since he had diarrhea from all the curry). Popi fell off the elephant, was concussed, and didn't make the third and fourth services, so he couldn't give away the bride another two times. Ohm got scabies from a bitch in heat down by the river. Endi and Coleman discovered an Indian titty bar, bought it, and missed all four services, for which Padme forgave them (of course). Zio was the best man all four times—four diamond rings.

Padme was barren. (She was much older than she looked.) She and Guido adopted sixteen Somali orphans and purchased four nubile Haitian nannies to take care of them from an agency operated by Ignacio—who started this whole thing. (Remember him, formerly of Fort Lauderdale and his mother in Haiti; he scuttled the *Master Baiter*?) The young girls were smuggled into Florida by an airboat tourist outfit in the Everglades (a full-blooded Seminole and his D-cup, ex-stripper, ex–college student wife—remember her?). The team continues to this day helping place other refugee children in nanny positions all over the world.

$ $ $

Shortly after being married, Padme and Guido purchased an island in the Bahamas. They also purchased the Universal Church of California. Retreats are offered on the well-developed island monthly; every month honoring another religion. The monthly schedule for the upcoming year starting in January is animism, February is Chinese folk religions, then shamanism, Sikhism, tribal religions, Baha'i Faith, Scientology, Mormonism, Jainism, Zoroastrianism, Caodaism, and finally (with a special New Year's Eve celebration) Wicca. They offer scuba diving, paddleboarding, water skiing, jet-ski rentals, parasailing, blue water fishing, a water park, a nine-hole golf course (all sand trap with every green on its own island surrounded by water that you can cool off in), a casino, swimming with dolphins, and a Michelin four-star French restaurant, as well as Jamaican, Mexican, and Italian restaurants, and a Wendy's. And, of course, a world-class beach. The ten-thousand-square-foot Cristal Temple of the Bahamas was built to be used by all faiths.

Padme has written sixteen books. Guido serves as her publicist, confidante, and travel coordinator. He also manages (his salary is a modest $3K a day) their controlling interest in the mattress business (now non-profit: they supply mattresses at no charge to any homeless shelter that asks). Padme has speaking engagements and séances all over the world. To date, she has only had one (serious) failure in her spiritual quest. That was a fire-walking retreat in Bora-Bora. She was evacuated to a specialist in Costa Rica who besides the burn management also did a thorough whole-body re-vamp (she was under anesthesia on and off for two days). Padme wrote her best-seller after that experience: *God Works in Mysterious Ways: How I Survived My Trial by Fire and Came Out a Better-Looking Woman.*

Ohm has the run of the island, of course, and is the darling of the dancing girls and kitchen(s) staff. He unfortunately has gained considerable weight and has to go to the mainland once a month for fatty liver flushing.

He has bilateral cochlear implants. He has had both lenses of his eyes replaced because of diabetic cataracts. (He is quite light sensitive and has to wear very dark wraparounds whenever he is outside.) He pulls a small oxygen tank and insulin pump with him everywhere he goes. All of his teeth are implants and now his gums are quite healthy again, and he regained his voice. He has his own line of pet food (which he refuses to eat). He goes to Fort Lauderdale every two weeks with Padme on the company's pink Citation (Udder Air), when she has her hair done, to the pet spa (owned by the Tightwad Group) for his medicated soapless/non-detergent bath and coat dye and set, anal gland expression and packing, ear plucking, manicure, under-the-tail hygienic trim, and flushing of his prepuce (for chronic balanoposthitis). He has 877 kids and grandkids (that he knows of). His breeding days are over as his prostate is toast; he has to wear a truss to bed. His favorite T-shirt (Harley-Davidson) in his extensive wardrobe says: *Bitches Love Me*. He dreams of India regularly.

$ $ $

Ready Sloan works for Coleman and Endi. She and the Conch Island Haitian brothers, who move mattresses for Padme, (Prince Jey Jey and Shelove Robert) operate the New-Stiltsville Social Club and Marina in a protected cove on the Universal Church of California's (UCC) island in the Bahamas. It is non-profit (proceeds go to the UCC). Among many things offered, the club specializes in exotic drinks (Down There, Love Tunnel, Coozie, and Hoo Hoo, for example), and pulled pork and Jamaican chicken sandwiches (Pork Sword, Tonsil Tickler, Jack-in-the-box, Dick and the twins, to name a few), and romantic "serious-fling" lodgings, and pan-cultural exotic dancing training. The three entrepreneurs oversee their Stripper-of-the-Month-Home-Visit Clubs in South Beach, Orlando, Pompano, and Fort Meyers on the East Coast, and Portland, Salem, and the Deschutes National Forest on the West Coast. They closed the one in Key West because there were so many naked people running around already that there was no market. (Franchise opportunities are available. 1-UTAKEITOFF.)

$ $ $

The assistant purser on the *Ecstasy* checked on Bond (James Bond) shortly after Shawn and Jason departed the ship with Taco Udder via helicopter. He helped Bond (James Bond) out of his restraints and found him some clothes. He and Bond (James Bond) now operate a bar called Cupid's Fling in Key West. Their patrons are mostly cross-dressers and transvestites. The extremely successful business partners have served as co-mayors of the annual Key West Fantasy Fest in October two years in a row, and every year they lead an excursion (two Prevost RVs–full) to Burning Man, Labor Day weekend, in Nevada followed by another week in Reno. They also are part owners of Conch Island Same Sex Marriage Company.

$ $ $

The Riviera, and sixteen other hotel, apartment, and boat-liveaboard complexes in Fort Lauderdale were purchased by a holding company in the Turks and Caicos, an Australian/Chinese/Japanese non-profit consortium owned by the Spanish-Chinese-Nipponese Global Non-Profit Properties Corporation, which maintains P.O. boxes in Seoul, Yokohama, Taipei, Tokyo, Copenhagen, Tightwad, Missouri, and Nuuk, Greenland. The company provides racially diverse exotic dancer troops for Stiltsville and other worldwide venues. All the buildings and docks in the sixteen complexes were renovated and deeded in perpetuity to be used only for liveaboard boat owners, and the buildings, as hotel rooms and apartments. Many have been declared national historical buildings and given reduced or tax-free status. (The crew bought a law firm that specializes in non-profits and is a non-profit.)

$ $ $

Jason, Shawn, and Taco bought the Lightningbolt Marina and Lounge for back taxes on the Broward County, Florida, courthouse steps. The transaction was bankrolled by the Tightwad Bank and Trust under the condition that the marina become non-profit. They painted everything pink. It ended up being a lesbian mecca to the great surprise of Shawn and Jason who, of course, went with the flow as always. They used the vast proceeds from its immensely successful operation to import several gifted surgeons and specialists from Costa Rica who they set up in a non-profit hospital in a former nursing home on Las Olas in Fort Lauderdale that the Tightwad Bank and Trust had foreclosed on. The center now specializes in surgery of the breast, vaginal and anal neuromuscular salvage, anal bleaching, and enhancements and reductions of all kinds. They have started a medical school on Conch Key, the dean of which is a Chinese world-renowned sex-change surgeon (male to female).

Jason, Shawn, and Taco also co-sponsor the increasingly popular cigarette boat race to Bimini every year for breast cancer awareness. All female drivers (no males allowed) are to drive naked, except for flotation devices. The entire island of Bimini is taken over for the lesbian-only three-day weekend event. Jason and Shawn are the only males allowed (other than gay men servers posing as Roman eunuchs) and the two are ceremoniously carried on their thrones to the opening and closing ceremonies by large, oiled girls dressed as Amazon warriors. A lottery is sold daily, and drawn nightly, for bisexual girls to have the chance to service the two guys. Jason and Shawn (reluctantly) participate as the girls are all disagreeable, bossy, and generally horridly ugly. (Business is business.)

$ $ $

Taco donates her considerable spare time and her helicopter(s) to the Civil Air Patrol of Florida and flies search and rescue operations over the Everglades and offshore. In the heart of the Everglades, she rescued a man that was emaciated and matted-haired and bearded to his navel. He was wearing only a Dolphins' football helmet, a woman's faded green bikini bottom, and a cape the size of a pup tent made from several distressed-beyond-recognition beach towels roughly fastened together by zip ties.

Taco and the paramedics were only able to understand bits and pieces of whatever language he spoke. He claimed to have been dropped there by a hurricane (with his mattress). At first, she thought he might be an Aztec—he was burned red and brown and had a strange talisman around his neck.[12] It looked like every square inch of his body had been tortured or was three square meals a day for insects for the last ten years. He would not leave without his mattress. Taco had to bungee it to a skid. She took him to the facility and surgeons at the Tightwad Ebenezer Reformed Baptist/Episcopal Surgery and Rehab Institute, Spa, and Buddhist Prayer Center on Las Olas in Fort Lauderdale (non-profit managed by the Tightwad Group). Guido arranged for a new mattress as a gift from the Sealy Corporation (owned by the Tightwad Group and now a 501c3).

When they had done all they could, he was permanently committed to the Florida State Hospital in Chattahoochee. He insisted his name was Levitra, which everyone thought hilarious, especially since he had a hard-on half the time which he stroked obsessively. He'd found a bicycle horn,

---

12 On examination by the emergency room nurse-practitioner, the "thing" around the individual's neck was found to be a dog anti-bark training collar (flesh had grown around it). It was discovered that the faint ozone, metallic, and burned rubber smell it emanated acted as an alligator and snake repellant and contributed to his survival. After an article published in the *New England Journal of Medicine*, many working in the Everglades now wear electronic dog shock training collars over sleeveless turtleneck dickies.

which he would not let go of, and honked it incessantly to the continued agony of the staff and other patients. He never once ventured outside again.

He died wearing his helmet and honking his horn as he reached for the light.

$ $ $

Coleman asked Endi, "Do you want another?"
"Is a fifteen-pound parakeet fat?"
"I'll take that as a yes."

I appreciate you reading my book!
Can you leave a comment and a star rating
on Amazon?

Sign up on my website to see my other books:
www.jarviswrites.page.
(We promise not to abuse your time and
will only notify you once or twice a month of specials
or pet food–related warnings.)
The website is loaded with pet food recipes
and pictures.

There are four books coming soon
similar to *Dirty Money*. The next one is called *A Rum
With a View* and introduces the Detective Johnny
Walker Investigations series.

Other non-fiction books by Jarvis include:
Feeding Your Dog and Cat, The Truth!
(I am a veterinarian) and an easy read, *Prayer Lite*.

Join my launch team and get my books for free
before they are published!!